REPOSITIONING

LOST LOVE, FOUND

JEANINE LAUREN

Repositioning: Lost Love, Found was first published in Canada and around the world by Jeanine Lauren. This is a work of fiction. Similarities to real people, places or events are entirely coincidental.

ISBN 978-1-7388343-0-3

To all those who have inspired me to travel, whether by plane, train, automobile, boat, foot, or armchair. It has expanded my life and I am grateful.

CHAPTER 1

Maria Phillips was ten deep in line to drop off her luggage at the Charles de Gaulle airport in Paris when her cellphone rang. She looked at the call display and smiled when she saw the picture of a smiling woman with a classic brown bob. Her sister had been using this photo ever since Maria had taken it five years ago at Cynthia's daughter's graduation.

"Cynthia? Hi. Have you already arrived in Florida? Are you excited about the cruise?"

"That's why I'm calling," Cynthia said, her voice tinged with regret. "I'm not coming."

"What? What happened? Did you miss your flight?" Maria's shoulders slumped and her tote bag slid down her arm.

"No, no, nothing like that. Um."

"What happened?" Maria demanded. It sounded like Cynthia was upset, but with the ambient noise in the airport, it was hard to tell. Maria pressed the phone to her ear and listened to her sister's voice for any clues.

"It's Gerrard. I can't leave him right now."

"What's wrong with Gerrard?" Her brother-in-law had been as strong as ever when she saw him two years earlier. Had it really been two years?

"I." There was a crack in her voice revealing Cynthia was holding back tears.

Maria hoisted her bag up onto her shoulder with her free hand. "What? Tell me. I can't help if I don't know what's wrong."

"I'm worried he has dementia or something. Since he retired, I've noticed he's forgetting so many things. I need to go with him to his medical appointments. He has tests booked."

"Why haven't you told me this before? We talk every week." Maria had made a point of calling Cynthia on Sundays wherever she was in the world. This was the first she had heard of any concerns about Gerrard.

"You know how private a person he is," said Cynthia. "I felt I would be betraying him if I said anything. And until now, I thought I could handle things alone. I didn't want to bother you. I..."

Maria noticed the line moving in front of her and pushed her suitcases forward.

"Tell me what exactly is he forgetting? Why are you so concerned? Has the doctor said anything?"

"He's forgetting names, dates, keys. He forgot to put on his socks the other day."

"He's been under a lot of stress, though." Maria watched a family of seven step up to the check-in desk and slid her bags forward again. Only two people ahead of her now. "You said he's been having trouble with retirement, trying to find meaning. Are you sure he isn't just depressed?"

"I don't know," Cynthia sounded exasperated. "The doctor is sending him to a specialist for tests next week. I have to go with him. And, if it is depression, well, I have to be here for him. He's my husband."

"I still don't understand why you've said nothing until now. Surely, you've known about the specialist appointment for a while. Or did they get him in on an emergency?" There was a tap on her shoulder and Maria looked up from the spot on the floor she had focused on while trying to puzzle out what Cynthia was saying to see she was next in line. She stepped back and put her hand over the receiver. "You go first," she said to the couple behind her. They had a mountain of luggage and three kids in tow. The woman nodded gratefully, and they all filed past. Maria turned her attention back to her conversation. "Sorry, Cynthia, I missed that. How long ago did he get the appointment for the tests?"

"Three weeks ago," Cynthia whispered into the phone.

"Three weeks! Why didn't you tell me sooner? I could have changed my travel plans." Cynthia didn't answer, and Maria noticed the people watching her. She was being that person. The one who was talking too loudly on the phone in public and holding things up. She glanced at her watch and waved to the next person in line to step ahead of her.

"Why would you wait until now to tell me?" she whispered into the phone.

"I've been worried about Gerrard. I lost track of time."

"Are you sure this isn't just an excuse not to come?" Maria asked, knowing her sister was afraid to travel on her own, afraid to try things that were out of her comfort zone.

"What? No! I fully intended to come but..."

"But? We haven't seen each other since Barcelona two years ago."

"I know," said Cynthia. "I wanted to come, but I can't right now. I'm really worried about him. Besides, I'll see you when you get to Victoria. The ship will be here in just over two weeks. By then, I will know more about Gerrard's health."

"Is that why you insisted on taking this repositioning cruise? So I would have to visit Vancouver Island? You know I don't want to come back."

"Not even if I need you? He's not well Maria. I need you to come home and help me."

"Like you helped me when Evan was dying?"

"Maria, that's not fair. You know how much I was going through then with Sabrina's graduation, and all the driving I was doing for Brad's soccer team? And I work full time, you know. You weren't working."

"Oh, I was working. Being someone's care partner is a full-time job." Though she would do it all again. Her husband had needed her. Evan would've done the same for her. She waved the next person in line to pass her by, then stepped firmly to the front of the line again.

"Are you serious about not staying when you get here?" asked Cynthia.

"I have another cruise booked. Eleven weeks through the Suez Canal. Remember?"

"Can't you put it off and come home?"

"I am home."

Cynthia sighed. "Traveling the world and living on a cruise ship isn't home, Maria. It's perpetual travel. You need to come home to your roots."

"So, I can look after you?" Maria immediately regretted saying what she'd been thinking.

"No. Not exactly. But I could use your support."

She saw the woman at the check-in desk wave at her and before she was tapped on the shoulder again, she said, "I have to go. I'm at the airport and have to check in."

"I'll see you when you get to Victoria and we can talk," said Cynthia. "I'll have more information about Gerrard's condition then."

"Sure."

"And let me know when you get on the ship."

"Yeah. Goodbye Cynthia." Maria clicked off the phone and walked up to the check-in counter, handed over her passport, and hoisted her bags onto the scale.

"Maria Phillips?" said the woman at check-in. "Good news, we can accommodate your upgrade request. I understand you want to use points?"

"Oh, that is good news," said Maria. She had not been looking forward to sitting in the middle seat for the ten-hour flight.

"Here you are." The flight attendant handed over

the boarding pass, then pointed toward the security gate.

Maria thanked her and walked in the direction the woman had shown her. Once she'd passed through the scanners and walked to the gate where she would board her plane, she sat down and pulled out her phone again to text her friend Belle who often traveled on the same ships Maria sailed on.

Maria: What time are you getting to Lauderdale?

Belle: About ten tomorrow morning.

Maria: I'll meet you on the ship then. Have a good flight.

Belle: Look forward to meeting your sister. See you there.

Maria didn't bother correcting Belle. She would save that information for later.

A short while later the announcement came over the loudspeaker calling for priority boarding, and she was soon settled into her seat, a pod where she could have a peaceful flight. She would worry about Cynthia and Gerrard later. Right now, all she wanted to do was get some sleep. She closed her eyes only to open them when she heard a piercing scream.

"Sorry," said a woman holding a baby who was taking the pod beside her. "She's a little tired. She'll be asleep soon."

Maria nodded and took the package of foam earplugs the woman handed to her. "Just in case."

"It's okay," said Maria. "I remember traveling with my daughter when she was younger. Starting her young will pay off in the long run." She thought back to the first time she and Evan had taken Haley on a trip to Mexico when Haley was three. She grimaced a little at the memory and, as she put earplugs into her ears, decided not to tell the mother sitting next to her that Haley had cried for two of the five hours they had been in the air.

She should call Haley. It had been nearly two weeks since they last spoke, but with the time difference, Haley would be asleep now. She would call when she got to Florida, which was in the same time zone as Ontario, where Haley lived.

Maria tried closing her eyes again but memories of her conversation with Cynthia bubbled into her mind. Cynthia sounded alone and lost, feelings that Maria knew all too well. Cynthia wanted Maria to come home, settle down, and be there to support her. But that would mean returning to Sunshine Bay where Maria had only memories of loss, and pain, and grief.

Traveling had kept those feelings locked away. Every day she met new people, saw new places, learned about different cultures, and made new friends, like Belle, who also lived the nomadic sea life.

Going back to Sunshine Bay would mean remembering every day that Evan was gone. She would see him in the local park where they often walked, on the beach, and, of course, in the home they had shared for thirty years. It would mean returning to see Haley's old bedroom and experience again the loss she felt when Haley had left the island five years earlier to live halfway across the country. Maria would have to start again to make friends that weren't part of couple groups because the couple groups had vanished one by one when Evan died. No one wanted a fifty-one-year-old widow tagging along.

No, she didn't want to go home. She wanted to keep moving like a rock rolling downhill. Away from the mountain of grief that awaited her when the ship she would board tomorrow sailed back to where she'd begun her travels three years earlier.

Now all she needed to do was make Cynthia understand that and to stop trying to make her come back.

~

Fourteen hours later, Maria found herself in line again, but knew this time it wouldn't take nearly as long. One benefit of having lived on cruise ships for three years was that she had earned priority status and upgrades. She would have a suite this time, something she had arranged because her sister was traveling with her. Make that, would have been traveling with her.

"Mrs. Phillips, I have a message for you," the woman checking her in glanced up from the computer screen. "I'm sorry to advise you that the ship scheduled to go to the Suez Canal next month was in an accident this morning."

"What?" Maria said. "What does that mean?"

"I am afraid it means we have canceled your voyage, but there is an agent on board who can assist you to book another cruise or arrange your refund. I'm sorry."

Maria stood staring at the woman. What did this mean? "There isn't a replacement boat? I booked this trip months ago."

"I realize that," said the agent. "But it is beyond our control."

"Thank you," said Maria, then hiked her tote bag higher on her shoulder and walked onto the ship. If she couldn't get another trip booked before this trip through the Panama Canal ended in Vancouver,

Cynthia might just get her wish. Maria may have a longer stay in Sunshine Bay than she liked, and she would probably have to stay with Cynthia as her house had long-term tenants. What was she going to do now?

A HALF-HOUR LATER, Maria stepped onto the stateroom balcony and folded her arms on the railing. She leaned forward to watch the last few passengers stop to have their picture taken by the cruise ship's photographer before walking up the gangway into the bowels of the ship below.

Heat emanated off the Florida pier, and she was grateful for the breeze gently ruffling her long silvering hair and playing with the hem of her ankle-length aquamarine cotton sundress. It was pleasant out here, away from the turmoil of passengers boarding, searching for their cabins, and exploring the ship. And quiet. She appreciated the quiet and hoped she didn't have to hear another baby cry for a very long time.

Most days on ship, she enjoyed sitting in the café area or in the lounge, people-watching, but today she would wait until the members' cocktail party that was given to those in the cruise line's loyalty program. She might as well go—this would be her last cruise for a while if she couldn't find a new booking.

There was a knock at the stateroom door, so she stepped inside and opened it to Belle, a petite forty-eight-year-old woman, three years Maria's junior, who had been traveling on the same ships for the past two and a half years and who had been Maria's fun-loving companion, always inviting Maria along on excursions and new adventures. Belle made living on a cruise ship feel like every day was an adventure and had helped her really embrace the nomadic life.

"You got rid of the pink, I see." Maria nodded toward Belle's dark-brown corkscrew curls shot through with electric-blue highlights. Belle was wearing a sarong of the same blue, splashed with bright yellow flowers. "I like it."

"I needed a bit of a change." Belle patted her hair. "Are you ready to go to the safety check? Where's Cynthia?"

"Oh, it seems I am sailing solo again after all. Cynthia couldn't make it. Her husband isn't doing well, so she couldn't leave him."

"Sounds serious." Belle said. "Is he okay?"

"Early days, from what I can tell. I'll know more

when I see her in Victoria when the ship lands there. So, meanwhile, it will just be you and me."

Belle searched her face as though trying to read her mood, so Maria pasted a smile on and said, "Right, let's go up and check in and get this over with. You would think we could get a pass on this by now, but they have their protocols." Maria checked to see that she was wearing the lanyard that held her cruise pass, then stepped into the passage and the stream of people flowing toward the outer deck to check in and find their muster station.

"There are a couple of hotties on board this one," Belle said, nodding toward two men in shorts and tight T-shirts walking toward them.

"Pace yourself," Maria said, squeezing Belle's arm and shaking her head. "You have two weeks to get to know them."

Belle chuckled and slowed her step, smiling and saying hello to the men before turning back to Maria. "You can never start too early on these things."

"You are incorrigible."

"And that's a bad thing?" Belle laughed and picked up speed. "We'd better get this over with, then grab lunch. I'm hoping for crab cakes today."

"And you can tell me about the conference," said Maria. "Have you checked in yet?"

"No, but I will. I'm excited and terrified. Excited that I get to teach at a travel writers' conference that is being held on a ship, but I'm also terrified I'll screw up. It's not like I can give a talk, then walk away and get on a plane. These folks are all on the ship with us for the next eighteen days."

"You'll do fine," said Maria as they stepped out onto the deck, found their muster station, held their passes out to be scanned, and instructed to listen to the safety briefing in their rooms as soon as possible.

"Let's get lunch first," said Belle. "Then I have to check in again with the cruise agent to plan my next trip. I still can't believe the ship we were supposed to board was in an accident."

"I'm not sure what our options are going to be. I imagine most trips are full by now. It was supposed to start in three weeks." That familiar feeling of dread rose to her chest, and she concentrated on pushing it away. She would not ruin this trip by dreading what would come next.

"I sent a note to my travel agent when I saw the news clip about the accident on TV. They are looking for something for me," said Belle when they got to the salad line. This was their go to lunch, salad from the salad bar and then, if still hungry, they would try the soup.

"I will try after lunch, though I'm not holding much hope. Maybe I'll see if I can get a cheap all-inclusive in Mexico or something."

"Or you could go and see your sister. Make sure she's doing okay."

"I could. I just really don't want to go back."

Belle placed her hand on Maria's arm and Maria turned to look down into her friend's serious face. "Sometimes we have to do things we don't want to do but are good for us, Maria. Maybe this is one of those things that will be good for you?"

"You sound just like my sister." Maria gently removed Belle's hand from her arm. "I'll think about it, Belle. Meanwhile, let's get our food and you can tell me more about the conference."

Maria stepped forward to tell the buffet server what she wanted on her salad, and told Belle she would find them a table, then set off. She needed to keep the focus on the present and hope that the cruise agent could help her rebook something else. She wandered around the buffet area looking for a table and finally spied a couple getting up from one near the window. While she waited for the server to clear it and bring her cutlery, she gazed out the window at the sea gulls diving and swooping nearby. Going home would be like putting one of those gulls in a cage.

Gulls were meant to fly.

When Belle finally joined her, she said, "You scored a great table. Good work."

"Years of practice," said Maria, picking up her fork to stab at a cucumber slice.

"I pulled up the updated conference schedule from the website this morning. There's a reception after dinner where I'll meet some participants and the other presenters. Do you want to be my plus-one? If it weren't for you, I wouldn't even have known about this opportunity. It's already boosted my Instagram account by a couple of hundred followers, and I've connected with three sponsors who might partner with me. I have a great feeling about it."

"I'm glad it worked out," Maria said. She had seen the advertisement for The New Horizons Travel Writers' Conference in a blog she followed, but when she'd mentioned it to Belle, she hadn't expected her friend to follow through and put in a proposal to teach travel blogging basics and monetization. Maria had been the one-person audience for the past several weeks while Belle honed her presentations. "And yes, I would love to be your plus-one."

"There are a few photographers speaking, and

some reps for travel magazines. I'm sure I could get you into some of the sessions if you wanted to come."

"Maybe. I'll look at the schedule and let you know."

"You should do more with your pictures. You have a great eye. You could sell them."

"I just dabble," said Maria. "It's something I used to do when I was in high school. Before Evan. Before..."

Belle put her arm around her and gave her a quick hug. "I'm sorry. I didn't mean to upset you."

Maria shook her head. "No, don't worry. You said nothing wrong. I've been getting pressure from Cynthia and it's bringing back memories, that's all."

"What kind of pressure?"

"She wants me to come home for good. She is really worried about Gerrard."

"If she canceled her trip, it must be serious," Belle said.

"I suppose."

"And do you miss her?"

Maria paused a moment before she answered. "I miss her, but I don't miss the town. Unfortunately, it's all mixed together."

"There must be something you liked about

Sunshine Bay. People come from all over the world to visit Vancouver Island."

"It's a quintessential small town on an island surrounded by natural beauty. What's not to love? It's just that it also reminds me of how much I've lost over the years. But let's not talk about that. Where are you planning to go next?"

Belle looked down at the deck. "I have a friend in Ontario who has been after me to visit for a long time."

"Oh. I see." Maria felt that familiar feeling of loss. "And you want to go."

"I do." Belle looked up at her, guilt flashing across her face.

"Then you should do it," said Maria. "It'll be an excellent opportunity, like this conference."

Belle looked relieved. "Thanks, Maria. You're such a good friend. But we'll keep in touch and find a time to meet up to do the Suez trip together. I don't want to miss it."

"You have other plans after Ontario, then." Maria's throat closed on the last word. She had always known she and Belle would eventually part ways, but it was too soon. Too sudden. When the ship docked on the island, she would truly return to the life she left behind and it made her want to cry.

"I have a couple irons in the fire," Belle said, not meeting her eyes. "But I don't want our travels to end. Let's find an alternate cruise through the Suez for some time in the fall, then put a deposit down on the trip tomorrow. Okay?"

"Okay," Maria injecting a note of cheer into her voice. "I would hate to break us up for long."

"I'm sorry to bail on you like this," Belle said. "But it isn't forever."

"We've always said today is the most important day."

"It's true. And whatever you decide to do...well, just do what's right for you, okay?"

"I will," Maria said. "And since this is our last trip together for a while..."

"Let's make it a good one," said Belle, lifting her coffee cup to toast Maria.

"Absolutely," said Maria, clinking her cup against Belle's.

CHAPTER 2

Nathan hoisted his backpack onto one of the single beds and briefly surveyed the cabin before leaning his crutches against the wall and limping back to the door to hold it open for his son, Rory.

Rory awkwardly pushed a wheeled suitcase through the door while pulling another behind him and past a pair of closets.

"Not bad," he said, leaving his burden in the middle of the room and walking toward the balcony to look out onto the waters below. "This will be a nice place to rest between sessions."

"And a far cry better than the last room we shared," Nathan said.

Rory laughed. "I'll never go to rural Scotland in

summer again. I still scratch when I think of the midges."

"In hindsight, we probably shouldn't have been tenting."

"And someone should have remembered to bring bug repellent." Rory glared good-naturedly at his father.

"I still think you were supposed to bring it," Nathan said. "And who was it that found the B and B when none were available?"

"Well, we now know why it was available." Rory made a face and shook a little. "It was nasty."

"But it kept most of the midges out."

"True enough. But it was nothing like this gig. Glad I could come along this time."

"Well, I needed someone to help carry my things." Nathan joked.

"You're saying I'm just a pack horse?"

"No. You'll also come in handy as a server," said Nathan.

Rory laughed. "Well, glad I can be of use."

"Have you spoken to Trevor?"

"Not yet. My phone needs to be charged."

"I'll text him then."

"It will be nice to visit him when we get to the

island. I haven't seen him since he moved in with Uncle Jake."

"Yes, it will be good to see him," said Nathan. "And the rest of the family of course."

At least it would be good to see his sister Sheila. It had been over five years since he was last home. He wasn't looking forward as much to seeing his brother Jake, but he only had to stay two weeks and then he would take off—provided his foot was better by then.

Today, though, his foot was throbbing. Even using a walking cast and crutches to keep the weight off, standing in line and boarding the ship had taken its toll. Two weeks ago, doctors had assured him it should be better within a fortnight, and that in a month, he would be able to go on another trek through Kenya for the wildlife charity that wanted his services. He just hoped he could make it. It was a great opportunity.

"Ever think of moving back this way again?" asked Rory. "Trevor has asked me to come and stay with him for a few months. I could travel around the island, blog, maybe even find a place to set up a studio."

And be closer to Ramona, their mother, thought Nathan. His ex-wife had just remarried and was living in Seattle, a boat ride away from Victoria.

"I'll think about it." Nathan said.

"It's not like you have anything keeping you in

Toronto anymore," said Rory. "You travel more than you stay in your condo. I bet you don't even know your neighbors."

"That's true. But having a home base in Toronto makes it easier to hop across the pond to Europe and Asia."

"But surely after your latest accident"—Rory looked pointedly at his father's walking cast— "you aren't actually going to travel a lot in the future."

"This?" Nathan waved at his foot with one hand while gripping the back of a chair with the other, working hard not to wince. "This is just a minor setback."

"Right." Rory rolled his eyes. "Six weeks in hospital, pins in your leg and foot, and four months of rehab... That is not what I call a minor setback."

Nathan glared at him. This injury would not keep him at home long. He would find a way to continue to travel and do what he loved to do: take photographs, tell stories through pictures, capture people's imagination and hearts, and, for the sake of the causes he supported, convince people to open their wallets to help.

"I'll see what the doctors say," he said. He would wait until he saw the orthopedic surgeon and physiotherapist in Victoria.

"Okay," said Rory. "But I'm not sure what you would have done if you'd been on that hike alone."

"Rory, I said I would think about it," Nathan growled. "Right now, I just want to sit down for a few minutes before we go to dinner. I'm tuckered out."

"I'm going to get some pics of the ship casting off," said Rory, putting his bag into the closet nearest to the door and grabbing his camera. "I'll be back about six to get you for dinner."

"Fine," Nathan grumbled to the door as it closed behind him. He pulled out his cell phone and texted his sister to say they had boarded and were on their way. Then he flipped his suitcase onto the bed, found the pain medication the doctor had prescribed him, unpacked his belongings and stored the empty bag in the closet. The entire operation took only ten minutes, but he was exhausted. Easing himself onto the bed and arranging his battered leg on a pillow, he settled back against another pillow and waited for the painkillers to kick in.

Rory had a point. With the boys both settling on the west coast and his ex-wife now remarried, there was nothing keeping him in Toronto. If he moved to the island, he could spend time getting to know Trevor better, and maybe reconnect with Jake.

Thinking of the effort involved in either of those

actions made him even more tired. He would just close his eyes a minute while he waited for Rory to return and for the pain to subside. He could feel his pulse in his toes as he dropped off to sleep, wondering if he would ever feel like himself again.

CHAPTER 3

After dinner, Maria took a few minutes to go to the main deck and check in with Yolanda, the cruise line's agent, to find out if there were any ships she could take to replace the canceled voyage.

As she waited in line, she glanced around the room and fingered the seashell in her pocket that always reminded her of Evan. The shell, which had become more fragile over the years from constant wear against her finger, was one of the few things she had taken with her when she escaped Sunshine Bay to travel. She'd intended to be away for a year, but one year had stretched to three, and unless she could find another trip soon, she wouldn't have a good excuse not to go back, see her sister, and face her past.

At the front of the line, she asked Yolanda again if she had found any options.

"I'm sorry, Mrs. Phillips," said the petite woman with a French accent. "It has been so busy since we spoke." She gestured to the line behind Maria that was getting longer by the moment. "But I will look again for some options."

Maria waited patiently for the flustered woman to do the search. Yolanda's brow furrowed as her fingers tapped furiously on the keyboard, but then she stopped tapping and glanced up at Maria, her look apologetic.

"I'm sorry, Mrs. Phillips. There isn't another ship leaving Vancouver when we arrive. This one will be doing the Alaska run all summer."

Maria's heart thumped hard, and she took a deep breath, fighting to keep her frustration from rising to the surface. It wasn't Yolanda's fault that she had taken this detour from Europe, nor that she had made the choice to come with Belle, thinking it would be interesting to compare a trip through the Suez Canal with this one through the Panama Canal. She had heard so much about both trips through fellow travelers over the years.

Yolanda was still waiting for instructions and glancing at the growing line of people behind Maria.

"Is there anything else I can do for you, Mrs. Phillips?" she asked. Maria looked hard at the woman, trying to keep tears from falling. Then she shook her head.

"No. I'll have to go decide what to do next. Thank you for your time." Maria picked up the book of cruise options from the desk and walked over to the nearby lounge where Belle was waiting.

"Well?" Belle looked up from her laptop and peered at Maria over reading glasses perched on the end of her nose.

Maria sat down as Belle pushed her reading glasses up on her nose again and returned her focus to the screen of her computer.

"No trips out of Vancouver next week except Alaska, and that's a round trip."

"What do you plan to do next?"

"I have no idea."

"Have you thought any more about visiting your sister awhile?" Belle leaned forward and looked at Maria more closely, as though interrogating her.

"Yes, I'll probably have to stay for a couple of weeks. The only trip out of Vancouver is this ship, and it's full."

"It sucks, but we can still do the trip. It may just not be right away is all."

"And it will give you time to see friends in Ontario."

Belle nodded, a shadow flowing over her face before she grinned again. "Yes, it's something I wouldn't have had the time to do this year if we hadn't taken this repositioning cruise."

"I haven't been this close to home since…" Maria swallowed hard, and Belle reached across the table to squeeze her arm.

"Coming this close is bound to bring back memories."

"It will be three years next month since he died. But sometimes it feels like only yesterday."

"What did your sister say when you told her they canceled the next cruise?"

"I haven't told her. I'm still looking for an alternative." Maria turned to a passing waiter to ask for a red wine and swung back to see a flash of disapproval on Belle's face. "What?"

"Not my business," said Belle, signaling to the waiter for another soda water with lime.

"And when has that ever stopped you? Say it."

"If you go there for a few weeks, you can assess the situation for yourself, lay her fears to rest, check in on your house, and if it gets too much, you can fly out to see your daughter. You haven't seen her since she joined us on the Christmas cruise."

Belle was right. She missed Haley and this would be a great time to visit her in Toronto. And it was an opportunity to check in on her property. Besides, Maria wasn't sure how she felt about truly traveling on her own again. It had been nice to have a companion along the way to share the adventures.

"Maybe you're right. It is time to consider going home for a few weeks. And I should spend more time with Haley. She's been distant since her father died."

"Dealing with ghosts head on is better than avoiding them," Belle said, and Maria tilted her head in agreement, though secretly wondered if that were true. Avoiding ghosts had been working for her so far. Keeping on the move, seeing new things and places every week, had kept thoughts of loss in the back of her mind, behind a growing wall of positive memories and experiences. If she stopped at home, the ghosts would have time to creep out again.

"The more I think of it, the better this idea seems to me," Belle said. "The weather is really nice this time of year on Vancouver Island, from what I know of it."

"Well, you'll see for yourself when we get to Victoria."

"I'm looking forward to it. I want to see where you grew up."

"It's different from Ottawa but in many ways the same. Both government towns."

"Except you don't have months of snow," Belle laughed. "I still remember reading about that snowstorm you had in the nineties. One snowplow for the whole city."

"I think the whole country was laughing at us that year," Maria said. "We had never seen so much snow."

"So, do you think you might stay on the island for a while? It would make me feel less guilty about breaking up our little duo, knowing you'll have something planned when I leave."

Maria looked her friend in the eye and took a deep breath. "I'll give it some thought."

"That's all I can ask," Belle answered. "Now, are you ready to come to the conference meet and greet? I think it'll be fun."

"Why not? It's always nice to meet other creative types."

They walked down the stairs to the lounge that had been reserved for the occasion, and after Belle introduced Maria to Cheryl, the organizer, she flitted off to mingle. Maria walked over to the long glossy bar and hoisted herself up onto a high stool to luxuriate in her favourite guilty pleasure of people-watching.

"Can I get you anything?" The bartender slid the drink menu toward her. She picked it up and glanced at it, though she knew it by heart. "Just a glass of white wine," she said. "A pinot." She pointed at the menu and then waited as he pulled the bottle from the shelf behind him and poured her a glass. She gave him her Sail Pass and signed the bill before climbing off the stool and walking to a lounge chair to watch the musicians set up for their next show. The buzz of conversation increased as people settled into the chairs around her to wait for the music to start and the servers navigated around tables, ferrying drinks. Maria listened to snippets of conversation around her. Where are you from? How many cruises have you been on? The usual questions travelers asked each other. Questions Maria found herself less and less interested in answering as time wore on.

She turned her attention away from the voices and listened to the singer, who had started crooning an old Frank Sinatra tune, "Fly Me to the Moon." What were her options? She could go to Europe if she could find inexpensive accommodation. That might be possible. It wasn't peak season yet. But she had already spent a lot of time there over the past year, and she was ready to go somewhere new. She could return to Canada and stay with friends in Vancouver, though explaining why she couldn't take the ferry ride home to Cynthia would be more trouble than it was worth. It was always the same old conversation.

"It's time to come home," Cynthia would say again. "You need to get on with your life. You're just running away from your responsibilities. Your family."

"I was responsible. Look what that got me: a husband who died in my arms, and a child who is grown, gone, and living her own life. There's nothing left in Sunshine Bay for me."

"You have me. You have friends."

"I have you. Yes. But you're busy with your own life, raising your own kids." And even in her imagined conversation, Maria couldn't tell her sister that she found her suffocating.

"You have hobbies."

"I had hobbies. And then Evan got sick, and it took all my time for two years to look after him."

"You can pick them up again."

"I did," she would answer. "I take pictures of all the wonderful things I've seen in the world."

"But you can't do that forever."

"Why not?"

"Because your family needs you. Your daughter needs you. I need you."

"And what if I don't want to be needed anymore? What if I just want to be free?"

And if she returned to Sunshine Bay she would be giving up on her freedom, and on Evan's dreams for her.

She took the shell out of her pocket and looked at it as though it were an oracle that could answer her dilemma. The shell felt like a part of Evan was still with her. Watching over her. Helping her through as he always had.

The day he had found it on the beach was during one of the last walks they took there together to watch the sunset. They had come upon a tide pool a bit deeper than normal and peered in to see the sea life continuing its daily routine in the tiny microcosm of ocean, waiting for the waves to return and free them.

"Look." He had grasped her hand and pointed. "A hermit crab."

In the deepening gloom, they had peered into the pool to watch the tiny creature. Its grey-blue legs and red claws poked out from under the dog winkle shell it lived in. It drew up alongside another larger shell, and Evan and Maria crouched, fascinated, as it hoisted itself from one shell to the other before trudging up the rocky outcrop in search of dinner.

"Did you see that? I wish I could do that."

"It would certainly allow us to avoid packing," she had said, laughing. "Until we started this downsizing exercise, I never realized how much stuff we owned." But he didn't return her laugh.

"What's wrong?"

He had leaned forward and plucked the old shell out of the water. "I went to the doctor this week," he said as he dropped the shell in his pocket. "They've confirmed that my trouble swallowing is the beginning. It's started."

Maria had remained crouched a moment longer, thankful for the dusk, so he wouldn't see her eyes fill with tears. They had known for years that he would probably develop symptoms before he was fifty. But when he passed his thirtieth, fortieth, and fiftieth birthdays, she had fooled herself into believing that the disease had skipped his generation. That just because his father and grandfather had died of ALS didn't mean he would. And there was always the hope for a cure.

"Maria?"

She had squeezed his hand as he helped her up.

"Well, we'll just make the very best of every day we get, then. And today has been a wonderful day."

"We need to tell Haley. It's time she knew."

"Okay, we'll fly out to Toronto for a weekend. She's been asking us to visit. I think she wants us to meet her new boyfriend. It sounds serious."

"I think it will be better if we send them tickets to come here," he had said. "I don't have a lot of time."

"But you must have years."

"No, Maria. I don't have that much time left, and I want to see my daughter before I leave."

What he didn't say that day was that he had already been talking to counselors, already decided on the date he would leave her. The day she would be left alone.

The twang of a guitar string grabbed her attention, and she swiped at her eyes as she refocused on the present and on a new group of players that had taken the stage and were tuning instruments. She looked at the shell again, but it held no answer to the question of where to go next. She didn't need to decide right away. The ship wouldn't dock in Vancouver for another two weeks. She may as well relax in the meantime.

The band started playing some rock and roll tunes from the fifties, infusing the air with a festive vibe. A pair of women moved to the dance floor to try out a jive, giggling at their missteps, while another cluster of women stood on the side of the dance floor, swaying to the music, and drinking in the sight of the handsome lead singer, a man in his fifties, she guessed, with a honeyed tenor voice and a smile that would make any woman's knees weak. A couple dressed in matching walking shorts and shirts began a quickstep at the corner of the floor, and she watched them, appreciating the way they moved in tandem, evidence of a lifetime partnership both on and off the dance floor. Her eyes misted, and she looked away. Evan had been able to lead even a rag doll through a waltz and make it look good. It was a skill she hadn't appreciated until he had passed, and she was left to sit on the sidelines, involuntarily tapping her foot to the music. Most of the men who came on board were married or partnered and didn't ask her to dance. But she did have Belle, who could lead as well as anyone, and often did when they were both in the mood to kick up their heels. Belle, who was now circulating around the room, enjoying herself.

She would miss Belle.

When she looked back toward the band, she sensed someone watching her. This wasn't unusual. Since being on her own, she had noticed it often.

Sometimes it was married women, sitting with their husbands and looking at her in what she imagined was triumph or pity. Or, in the case of those with frail older men in their company, fear. Fear of being alone soon too. Fear of change. Fear of their own mortality.

Sometimes the eyes were of men who had strayed from their marriage bed more times than they had been in it. Sometimes it was the eyes of widowers—usually recent widowers, because in her experience they didn't remain alone long. And sometimes it was bachelors. Confirmed or divorced.

Today she noticed a man sitting across the room glancing in her direction and then back at his cell phone. She shifted casually in her chair to get a better look. The last thing she needed was to encourage anyone at the beginning of a two-week trip. She'd made that mistake once. A recent widower had latched on to her and invited her along to all kinds of excursions until she felt stalked. He'd finally, thankfully, moved on to another woman who seemed to like him.

As she shifted toward the man, he bent over his cell phone, intent on the screen as though answering a text. His profile was familiar. Perhaps she had seen him on another cruise. She had run into a few travelers more than once, like she did with Belle before they began planning some of their trips together. She casually turned her head again to get a closer look. His hair was cropped short, mostly dark, but with a good amount of silver scattered through it. He looked to be tall, but she would have to wait until he stood to be sure. She picked up her wine and sipped it to calm her nerves. Why was she nervous? Men looking at her rarely made her feel anything except, occasionally, annoyance.

She considered the mystery some more. If she didn't know him from the ship, where did she know him from? One of Evan's workmates, perhaps? There were a lot of Canadians from Vancouver Island on the ship. It was a possibility. She ran through the list of men who had congregated at her home during Canucks games and struck them off quickly. None of them looked like the man across the room—and she would remember feeling twinges of attraction to a friend of Evan's, wouldn't she? Or maybe attraction was something that shut off when you had someone you loved. She hadn't noticed other men when Evan was alive. They had been too busy living their life together.

Where had she seen him before? She rubbed the shell with her thumb to calm herself down then placed it back into her pocket and casually leaned back in her chair to get a better look.

He frowned at his phone, and she quickly sat forward. She knew that expression. Could it be him after all these years? *No.*

She must be wrong.

Casually she glanced again, and just as she did, he looked up in the direction of the band. She nearly dropped her wineglass before quickly turning her attention back to the musicians. The dancers. Away from those intense brown eyes.

Nathan.

The last time she'd seen him he'd had longer hair that he was forever pushing out of his eyes, but it was him, and her heart skipped—though they hadn't seen each other since their last year of high school, since that phone call when he'd told her he never wanted to see her again. What was the selfish jerk doing here?

She had to leave.

Now.

She stood quickly, still gripping her glass, and scanned the room for Belle, who was holding court with several of the men attending the conference. Maria hurried over and whispered that she had to go and respond to her sister's email—an excuse Belle would accept with little question—and exited the room without a backward glance.

As she hurried toward the stairs and up to the internet lounge, she took a few deep breaths to calm her panic. She would have to face him sometime in the next two weeks, but now she could steel her mind, protect herself. She didn't enjoy how the sight of him made her feel, nor did she like that he made her remember things she hadn't thought of in years. So many firsts had been with Nathan. Their first high-school waltz, their first kiss, the first time he told her he loved her, the first time they made love.

She would instead remember the pain when he'd left after their fight. The pain of unreturned letters, of being left abandoned and vulnerable. But she would have to talk to him. She had to tell him she hadn't done as he asked. She couldn't.

She sighed as she settled into the chair in front of a computer and glanced around the nearly empty room to ensure she hadn't been followed. Though she knew this was only a small reprieve. She had to talk to him sometime. She just needed to make sure she was ready.

CHAPTER 4

When Nathan and Rory arrived at the reception for the New Horizons Travel Writers' Conference, Rory was vibrating with excitement.

"I haven't seen you this way since I dropped you off at college," Nathan said.

"There are a few bloggers here I've been following for years," Rory said. "There's even the woman who calls herself the Vagabond of the Seas. They said she caught this trip on purpose so she could speak here."

"Well, off you go and mingle, then. I'm going to sit down over there"—Nathan pointed toward some seats near the dance floor— "and answer some of my emails."

"Don't forget to connect with Uncle Jake. Trevor says he's been trying to get hold of you."

"Hard to forget." Nathan waved his phone in front of him. "I've been pinged every three minutes since we boarded."

Rory laughed. "I'm going to grab a beer. Want anything?"

"Just a soda water," Nathan answered. "With lemon."

"Nothing stronger, Dad? You're on vacation."

Nathan stared at his son and raised one eyebrow.

Rory laughed and backed away. "Okay, okay. Soda with lemon it is. And seriously, don't forget to answer Uncle Jake's texts," Rory admonished. "You know he just wants to see you."

Nathan didn't know that. In his experience, his family only ever texted him when they wanted something. But for Rory's sake, he said, "I'm on it," and flashed his phone as proof.

Nathan shook his head, put his phone back in his pocket, and turned his crutches toward the seating area while Rory went off to collect the drinks. Lowering himself carefully into a chair, Nathan wished he could grab another seat to rest his foot on, but the place was filling up with people and there were none nearby. He leaned back into the comfort, trying not to think about how much work it would be to get out again. Instead, he would enjoy his view of the dance floor, the band, and the bar where Rory was buying the drinks.

He fished his phone out of his pocket before his son returned and scrolled through to look at Jacob's last few messages.

Jacob was six years younger than Nathan and had a myriad of talents, including mechanics—he could make an engine sing a concerto—and making a home for himself, his wife Valerie, his three sons, who were now all in college, and now Trevor. He was also a gifted actor. Yes, Jake could make the best thespian jealous with one of his adult tantrums.

Jacob was the one who had moved with their father when he left their mother all those years ago. Jacob was the one who swore he got the short end of the family responsibility stick. Jacob was the one who had no idea what he was talking about.

He looked again at his phone. Nothing. Jacob was probably still mad that he and Rory had honored their commitments to the conference and taken a slow boat back to Vancouver Island instead of flying directly from Toronto. But he had booked this cruise months ago, had asked the organizers to include Rory, who was new to his field, and he would be damned if his brother's histrionics over his estranged father would allow him to pass up—for the third time—his opportunity to go through the Panama Canal.

He had passed on the trip twelve years earlier when his mother died, and he had to go to take care of her funeral and estate. The second time had been two years after that, when his marriage fell apart and he had to make sure Trevor and Rory were going to be okay. Instead of using his vacation to travel, he had moved back to Toronto and found work managing oil projects until Trevor went off to trade school and Rory to university. Then he had finally traveled and lived his dream of being a wildlife photographer. That is, until the hiking accident, when he fell ten feet and smashed up his leg. The injuries were relatively minor considering what could have happened, but the fall had been rotten luck, and might well affect his ability to continue doing the work he loved. But he would worry about that later. As he'd told Rory, he would seek medical expertise and do all the physio he could before he would give up.

He hadn't told Rory about his conversation with Jake earlier that day, either. Because he'd be damned if his father would impede the boy's dreams.

"He's sick, Nate. He wants to see you before he gets much worse. They say he won't last much longer."

"I'll be there in eighteen days," Nathan had told

him. In his experience, their father, now only seventy-eight years old, was a tough old bird who would live as long as his grandfather had. Ninety-nine.

"You're an ass," Jacob had said and hung up on him. Jacob was forever hanging up on him, though. Once he cooled off, they would be in touch again. Instead, Nathan texted their sister, Sheila, to see if she could tell him more about their father's status. If it was bad, he would arrange with the conference to get off at San Francisco and fly directly from there.

He's not great. Should have quit smoking years ago, Sheila wrote back. *But the doctors said that he's not getting any worse. He's stable, and the bypass operation won't be for another three weeks. You have time.*

Good. No immediate reason for concern. Sheila was the more level-headed of his two siblings. She had always been the peacemaker of the three, a skill likely learned through splitting time between their parent's houses after the divorce. She was the only one of them who had done that, though Jacob spent more time with their mother than Nathan had with their father, which hadn't been hard. Nathan didn't go where he wasn't welcome, and his father had made it plain more than thirty years ago that Nathan was not welcome in his home.

A familiar anger seized Nathan. An anger he

normally kept at bay. If it weren't for his father abandoning him and his mother, Nathan wouldn't have needed to find work in the oil fields out of high school. Instead, he could have gone to university and proved to Maria that he was good enough for her.

"Here you go, Dad," Rory startled him out of his musings.

"Thanks," he said, taking the drink from his son's hand. "I just texted Sheila. She says your grandfather isn't well." Rory's face fell, and Nathan hurried to reassure him. "But he's stable and on a list for surgery. If it were an emergency, they would try to get him in more quickly. His surgery is scheduled for three weeks from now."

"Good." Rory smiled again. "I'd hate to cancel and fly home, but I would if we needed to."

"I know you would. I'll keep in touch with Sheila and if things change, we'll fly back from Mexico or San Francisco. Now go and mingle." He shooed Rory away with his hand. "I'll try to get in touch with Jake now." He settled back into his chair and stared at his cell phone again.

A few minutes later, the band started playing "Blue Suede Shoes," and he glanced up when a couple gravitated to the dance floor. He watched for a few moments, wishing he could join them. Maybe by the end of next week he could dance a couple of tunes, though not if his foot ached like it had been doing all day.

He was about to look at his cell again when he saw a woman across the room watching him. Or at least he thought so. But when he looked back again in her direction, he could only see a head of long brown hair liberally streaked with silver. Just another conference-goer. Turning his attention to his phone again, he saw Jake had finally replied: *Fine. At least I know Rory will be responsible enough to bring you back with him. See you in two weeks.*

And that was all. He shook his head and looked up again. The woman looking in his direction looked just like Maria would if he'd known her today. His memories must have conjured up her doppelgänger.

The doppelgänger turned away from him as soon as their eyes met. How odd. Then she hurried to the far side of the room toward a woman with electric-blue streaks in her hair who was speaking to Rory. The doppelgänger was an excellent likeness. Her gait was the same as Maria's, as was the way she used her hands when she spoke. And when she exited the room, her back straight and her stride purposeful, he realized that this was no doppelgänger.

Of all the cruise ships on the seven seas, why did

she have to be on this one? And where was Evan? He considered rising to chase after her—he even reached for his crutches—but catching her up would be difficult.

And what would he do if he caught her? He needed time to figure out what to say when he saw her again. He would like to think he could be neutral, forgiving, even, like he was simply meeting an old classmate from school.

Anyone who knew him would laugh at that idea. The way he had felt about Maria could never be described as neutral.

He texted Trevor that they were aboard and on their way, and received a thumbs-up from his eldest son. That would be at least one positive outcome of his visit to Sunshine Bay. It had been over a year since he'd seen Trevor. He was looking forward to visiting and hearing how Trevor's apprenticeship was going. Meanwhile, Nathan would enjoy the cruise and, with luck, take some excellent pictures of the canal and countries they passed through.

And maybe, just maybe, he could learn the answer to the question he had been asking for decades. Why, only weeks after they'd broken up, had the woman he loved married someone else—and left his heart in tatters?

CHAPTER 5

While Maria waited for the computer to connect to the internet, she thought of Nathan again. How dare the man look so good after all these years? And how dare he still have the power to fluster her so much that she would run from a room to avoid him?

The login screen finally popped up and Maria drained the last of the wine. She pulled up the cruise website to look for trips that she could take, wishing she hadn't scheduled this trip around Cynthia's dates so she could have caught the Suez trip this month instead. *Cynthia.* The more she thought about the conversation with her sister, the more she wondered if this was just another ploy to have Maria return to Sunshine Bay. It was the same old song Cynthia had sung since the first day Maria had told her of her plans three years before, when she was visiting her sister for tea.

"You did what?" Cynthia had dropped her cup and let it roll on the carpet.

"Good thing that's empty." Maria had nodded at the cup. "You could have stained your new carpet."

"Forget the carpet. What're you thinking, Maria? Selling your house and running off to live on a cruise ship? Who does that?"

"I didn't sell it. I'm renting it out for a year at a time."

"A year! What will you live on?"

"Cyn, I have my survivor's pension, the money from Evan's life insurance, savings, and the rent money. I'll be fine."

"I can't believe you're running away like this. I know his death was hard, but seriously? Moving to a cruise ship for a year? At your age?"

That she would say that meant Cynthia could not begin to comprehend the depth of Maria's loss. His death hadn't been hard. It had broken her. She bit out the next words, in short staccato.

"Who do you think goes on cruises? People my age. And yes, I'm going for a year at least." *Whoops. Shouldn't have said that last bit.*

"At least!"

"It's not like I'm moving to Mars. I'll visit. And we can keep up through email. We've hardly seen each other over the last year, anyway."

"Is that why you're leaving? Because I couldn't help you look after Evan? And because I didn't support his decision to... well... you know."

"Check out on his own terms, you mean?"

Cynthia had nodded, but her face pinched as she tried to hold back the contempt that crept into her features whenever they spoke of Evan choosing an assisted death. Her sister would never understand what Evan had wanted to avoid, and Maria was tired of trying to explain his decision. And she was tired of this conversation.

"I'm not leaving because of that. I'm not trying to punish you. I just need to do this."

"I can't believe you're leaving just when I can finally see us spending more time together, when my kids are getting settled and my life is getting back to some kind of normal."

"Normal? Why is everything always about you? You think my life is ever going to be normal again?"

"Oh no. I didn't mean that. I wasn't thinking. I—"

"Don't." Maria had put up her hand to stop her sister's objections and apologies. They were the same objections Maria had raised to herself while she packed up the house. The house that was empty of Evan, empty of her belongings, but too full of their shared memories, joys, regrets, and losses.

“I’m going home to finish packing,” Maria had said. “I’ll come by in a few days before I leave.”

“I can’t change your mind?”

Maria had shaken her head, picked up her coat from the back of the kitchen chair, and walked straight out the door without a backward glance.

CHAPTER 6

She should check her emails. Even though she was still angry with Cynthia for bailing, she had to check in. Cynthia would be worried by now, and though a small part of Maria wanted to punish her sister for canceling on their plans, she couldn't bring herself to be so churlish. She leaned in to read the emails and sure enough, there were three from Cynthia with increasingly urgent subject lines: *Hi there*; *Where are you? Please respond as soon as you see this.*

Such drama. She picked up her wineglass to take a sip and grimaced when she remembered it was empty. Maybe she should go to the piano lounge later and get another. It felt like a two-drink kind of day.

She clicked on her sister's latest email.

. . .

Maria,

I'm sorry I had to cancel. I know you're disappointed. But what you don't know is that the tests are for Alzheimer's. I didn't think it was possible either, at first, but if you could see how much he has changed in the past year since he retired, you might understand.

Maria looked over at the empty glass, took a deep breath, and kept reading.

I am so scared about what they will find Maria, and I know you don't want to come home, but I'm hoping you can stay for a few days at least.

Please.

Cynthia

Perhaps she wasn't taking Cynthia's concerns seriously enough. Gerrard might really be sick, though it was difficult to believe that his barrister's mind for details would ever succumb to Alzheimer's. But she hadn't been home in three years, and she hadn't seen Cynthia and Gerrard since the cruise they shared out of Barcelona the previous year.

Maria thought back to that trip, and to a conversation they'd had their second day at sea.

"This is much more pleasant than I thought it would be," Cynthia had said.

"What did you expect?" Gerrard had asked.

"I don't know," Cynthia had said. "I guess I thought

it would be like the cafeteria at work—you know, with one place to get food and a couple of things on the menu. This is quite wonderful, to have so many options." She waved her hand around the room at all the food stations, where people were piling their plates high as they always did on the first few days of a cruise. "How do you stay so trim, Maria?"

"There are trainers on the ship, and I walk on the port days. Rarely ever miss a port day. There's just too much to see."

"Every day is a new adventure, eh?" Gerrard had taken another bite of his fluffy omelet.

"Exactly," Maria had said. "Enough to keep me in a lifetime of memories."

"When do you plan to come home?" Cynthia had asked. "I miss you."

Home? Maria *was* home. Without Evan to anchor her life to the land, staying adrift felt right.

"Are you kidding?" Gerrard had asked. "Soon you won't have time to miss her." To Maria he said, "She's already planning our next trip. When will you be going to France? She wants to join you then."

"I'll have to look at my schedule. I'm planning to do a trip to Australia this fall. Then I want to see South America. "

"Really?" Cynthia's eyes had lit up. "If you get me

the dates, I'll see if we can join you on the Australia trip. Oh, Gerrard. We can, can't we?"

Gerrard had laughed at the earnest look on her face, that look Maria had known since they were children. Her little sister, always the family darling, would use that look to convince their parents to let her have the big chocolate rabbit or, later, the keys to the car. Cynthia still had a knack for getting anything she wanted. For Maria, by contrast, the look usually meant more work for her. *Maria, make sure your sister doesn't eat too much of the bunny... Cynthia, you can go if Maria goes along to make sure you get home safe.*

"Thanks a lot, Mom," she muttered, clicking *reply*. Those early expectations were why she felt responsible for her sister even now.

Her response was quick, just to say she was on the ship and on her way to Vancouver and that she would connect again tomorrow. Meanwhile, she asked her sister to keep sending news—and not to borrow trouble, as their mother had always said.

She scanned her email again, looking for Haley 's name, and was pleased to find a note down at the bottom of the lengthy list. She really needed to weed out the mailbox and unsubscribe from things, but on sea days, she often enjoyed reading newsletters and blogs and catching up with what was happening in the world.

Hi Mom,

I have some fantastic news to share, and since Aunt Cynthia says you will be moving home now, I am so happy about the timing.

What? She wasn't moving home. Why would Cynthia tell Haley that?

Are you ready? Here it is.

Lance has asked me to marry him, and we're moving to Victoria. I am so excited! And I have more news, but I want to tell you in person. Or at least over the phone. I can't wait to see you. We'll be there in two weeks! Maybe even meet your boat if you send me the details.

Love you,

Haley

Maria stared at the screen and reread the message. Haley was getting married. Haley was moving to the island. Cynthia had told Haley that Maria was coming home permanently. And now Nathan was here.

Her world of adventure and no responsibilities was colliding with her world on land and Maria couldn't breathe.

She signed off the computer, pushed herself out of the chair, and forced herself to walk toward her cabin so she could call Haley. The email she had received had been sent over twenty-four hours ago, and her daughter would be concerned by now. Since Evan died, Haley liked her to keep in touch more often.

After settling onto her balcony and breathing in the sea air, she dialed the number on WhatsApp.

"Hi, Mom. I was worrying about you."

"I was just in transit and hadn't been checking my email is all. I wanted to call you right away to tell you how pleased I am with your news. Congratulations! Tell me the details!"

"Well, it has been a pivotal week for us. First, Lance told me he had been applying for work in B.C, trying to get back to the island. I knew that. I mean, I've been applying for work there too, whenever I see jobs in community health. It's always felt like such a long shot, but this week he got a job in the oncology department in Victoria! He's been working for years for this, and he's always wanted to go back to the west coast."

"And what about you?"

"That's the best part! I was offered a job as a community health nurse. I wanted a job with shorter shifts, working with new parents, and out in the community. I start in three weeks!"

"And you've decided to get married too!"

"It was out of the blue, though I guess I should

have seen the signs." Haley giggled, which made Maria smile. Haley never giggled unless she was exceptionally happy.

"We went out to celebrate our jobs, our move, and he asked me to marry him in the park near our house. The one they use to take wedding photos. It was so lovely. He got down on one knee and everything. I nearly fainted, I was so excited!"

"How romantic." Maria smiled for her daughter. She liked Lance. He seemed responsible, kind, and he reminded her of Evan in so many ways.

"But that's not all, Mom."

"There's more than that?"

"I was going to wait to tell you this until I was further along, but I just can't. Mom, I'm pregnant. You're going to be a grandmother!"

"A grandmother?"

"I was so happy to hear you were coming home to the island. Aunt Cynthia says you will be staying once you land. Not traveling as much. We'll be a family again!"

"Congratulations!" Maria hoped she sounded excited. A grandmother. She hadn't expected that to happen. Haley had always been so career focused. But she supposed that at thirty-two, if she wanted to have a family, now was the time.

"Listen, Mom, I have to pick up Lance from the hospital. I'll talk to you soon, okay?"

"I look forward to it, and I can't wait to see you both. Love you."

"I love you too, Mom."

They ended the call, and Maria stared up at the stars. The moon was bright tonight, and the evening calm. She should have been pleased about the news. That her daughter was moving back to the island. That her little family was growing and would be together again.

But all she could focus on was Cynthia and her machinations. Why had she told Haley she would stay? How could Maria now tell Haley she would leave again as soon as she could? And now that Haley was going to have a baby, how could she leave again? The familiar squeeze of expectations gripped her around the middle, and she took a deep breath, trying to ward off that feeling of entrapment. Of obligation.

She stood to go inside. She needed to walk again, digest this information, think about what to do next—and how to talk to Cynthia when all she wanted to do was wring her ruddy neck. Contacting her could wait until tomorrow, to ensure she did nothing she would regret.

She opened the room safe and placed her phone

inside again. She was on a ship, she was going to enjoy the journey, and right now, she was going to find a second glass of wine to toast her daughter's happiness before going to bed.

It had been a long day.

CHAPTER 7

Maria made her way to the elevator the following morning, past the familiar ship walls papered in sapphire and silver and the chrome-and-glass fittings shimmering in the light. She knew the pomp and circumstance of the first few days was a careful façade designed to show people a fun time while parting them from their dollars, one fancy drink and exciting gemstone at a time. Longer-term travelers like herself would see behind the curtain in a few days: the rust spot here, the tear in the paper there, the server whose smile slipped as soon as he walked away. But most would happily stay oblivious to the details until they landed in Vancouver.

There was a lineup in the dining room, so instead Maria turned toward the cafeteria, where she could grab a quick bite. Today, she couldn't face strangers at the table she would need to share. She didn't want their questions. Where are you from? What do you do? How many cruises have you taken? She didn't want to share little truths with people she would never see again, people who would forget her existence once they landed and melted back into their regular lives. She knew she had become an anecdote people shared. We met a woman who has lived on ships for over two years. Isn't that fascinating?

Adventurous?

The saddest thing you've ever heard?

She wandered around the buffet and filled her plate with fruit and porridge, then took it and a fresh cup of coffee down to her cabin, where she turned on the television to see if she could find a movie. Music from *Pirates of the Caribbean* filled the room, and she watched the show with half her attention while she ate.

It was no use asking herself what she was going to do. She already knew the answer. She knew she would return home and stop traveling for a while. The question now was how she would return to Sunshine Bay without falling apart—and without becoming the family caregiver.

Outside, she could hear companions, friends, and

family talking in the corridor as they passed. The chatter of others made her feel lonelier than she had in months.

There was a knock at the door then, and she jumped up to answer it. Belle stepped inside, carrying a breakfast tray.

"I was hoping you'd be here. I couldn't face the usual first-day questions today, and after that reception last night, I'm tuckered out. Thought I would see if you were around before I went back to my cabin."

"You're just in time." Maria smiled and waved at the chair across from her.

"Have you decided about what to do next?" Belle asked as she sat and spread a napkin over her lap. She never was one to stand on ceremony, and she always said exactly what she was thinking. A benefit or a curse, depending on the day.

"I'm going to follow your advice and visit my sister for a few weeks. It will help me gauge the situation more closely and lend a hand if needed. She thinks her husband may have Alzheimer's."

"I hope that isn't the case. He's quite young, isn't he?"

"I think he's sixty-one. Several years older than Cynthia."

"No wonder she needs you. You're her only sister."

"I know. Don't make me feel any guiltier than I do already. I should probably just fly back now. The tests aren't scheduled until next week and it could take a week or more to get the results."

"And you aren't sure you're ready to face the memories yet." Maria flinched at Belle's direct stare. "Is that why you're eating in the room this morning?"

"That, and the need to digest the news I just received from Haley."

"Oh, do tell!" Belle's eyes widened.

"It seems that I am going to be a grandmother."

"Ohhh!" Belle squealed. "That's so exciting!"

"And Haley and Lance are getting married."

"So, you'll have a new son-in-law. You like him, so this just keeps getting better and better," Belle said.

"And..." Maria took another drink before she spit out the harder bit. "Lance and Haley have both landed jobs in Victoria. They're moving back to the island."

"Wow! That's a lot to take in."

"To top it all off, Cynthia has informed my daughter that I am moving home."

Belle's mouth dropped open. "You aren't serious. "

"Apparently she's determined to force me to come home, regardless of the cost."

"You must feel painted into a corner. How could she do that?"

"That's the way my sister is. She wants something, and she chips away at things until she gets it." Maria closed her eyes a moment, tempted to tell Belle the very worst of it, but she decided to wait.

"Enough about me," she said. "Tell me about the conference. Are you meeting some great contacts?"

Belle was startled by the change in subject but was soon regaling Maria with stories of the people she had met. "And there's a young guy on board, Rory, traveling with his father, who is a photographer at the conference. Rory says he's been following my blog for years. I thought it only appealed to an older crowd, but he enjoys reading about the adventures I get up to. It was what convinced him to attend this conference. That, and his father got him on as a speaker."

"You should give the cruise company that information. If you're drawing a younger crowd, maybe you could get a sponsorship or something."

"Maybe," Belle said, "though with the next cruise being canceled, I've been considering my options. I guess the unexpected itinerary change brought me out of the cruise trance."

Maria knew what she meant. It was easy to stay on the ship and pretend it was all there was to the world. Even the port visits were a part of the illusion. Like a virtual reality show where you stop in one port, explore for a few hours, and then rejoin the cruise world and sail off to another destination the next day.

"Sometimes I wonder if I should settle down somewhere now," Belle said.

"You, on land? I can't picture that."

"I wasn't always a seafaring nomad, you know."

"Where would you go? "

"I may go home for a few weeks. See my family. Reconnect. I think it may be time."

"Where is your family?" Maria asked and realized she didn't know the answer. In fact, she didn't know about Belle's family at all. Was she so self-absorbed that she hadn't ever bothered to ask? No, she realized. It was that Belle always managed to steer the conversation away from herself.

"I don't really have much family left." Belle was serious for a moment. "At least none who want to see me." Maria was silent. Waiting. Belle never let her guard down.

"I made some terrible mistakes when I was younger. My kids grew up to be strong despite me. They lived with their father and he, well, he cut me out of their lives and made it stick with a court order."

"I didn't know," Maria said. "Why have you never told me you had kids? "

"My losses aren't things I like to talk about."

Maria reached across the table and grasped Belle's hand. "I wish you'd said something."

Belle sat back, pulling away from Maria's grasp. "It was a long time ago. And I do keep tabs on them through Facebook—and the occasional email from an old friend who agreed to keep me informed without my ex knowing."

"What happened?"

"I lost custody. My ex has a lot of influence and he used it in the courts."

"I'm so sorry. You must think me so selfish, leaning on you when you were going through so much."

"Maria, I think you are a good friend who has been going through her own grief and pain. I never wanted to burden you. Besides, having you in my life for the past two years has kept me on the straight and narrow. You've been good for me."

Maria waved away the praise. "We've saved each other, I expect, and if you ever do want to land somewhere, let me know. Maybe we can find a place together. I have a house on the island."

"Be careful what you offer, my friend. You may be sorry you said that one day."

"After what we've been through together, I don't think so." Maria reached forward and grasped Belle's arm again. "I am serious, you know. If you ever need a place to call home, stay with me. I'm your family now."

"Thanks, Maria. I'm sorry I never told you about them. I guess talking about my children is still too hard."

"Where do they live? What are their names?"

"My sons, Leo and Logan, are twenty-five and still in Ontario, working on taking over the family moving business. My daughter, Tabitha, the youngest, is in Alberta. I'm not sure how she's doing. She hasn't kept in touch with my friend, and since my ex-husband remarried, my friend doesn't see him often."

"Are you ever in touch with them directly?"

"No. I've honored the demand that I stay out of their lives until my daughter is nineteen."

"How old is she now?"

"Twenty-one." She looked down at the plate in front of her and picked up her fork to spear a blueberry. "I know. I'm a coward."

"Not a coward. Just someone trying to get over a broken heart." Sensing her friend wanted to move on from the subject, she changed it. "Speaking of broken hearts..."

Belle looked up at her and raised her brow in question.

"My first love, who left me at eighteen to run off to the oil fields, is here."

"Where? You mean here on the ship?"

"I saw him at the piano bar last night."

"So, he's with the conference? What did you say to him?"

"I said nothing. I ran out of the room. I guess we're both cowards."

That brought a smile to Belle's face, and she laughed. "What a pair we are, eh? What are you going to do when you run into him again? It's bound to happen on such a long voyage."

"Well, for now I thought I would finish my breakfast then go up to the spa to see if I can use some of my credits. If I'm not going to be on board for a while, I may as well enjoy my sea days."

"If I weren't going to the conference, I'd join you," Belle said, taking a last drink of coffee and placing her napkin on the tray. "I love a great massage. But right now, I have to go. Want to meet for lunch?"

"Sounds like a great idea. I'll be hungry after all that pummeling and pampering."

Belle laughed and went to the door. "See you at noon."

CHAPTER 8

Nathan leaned on a desk at the front of the conference room and started his talk about the importance of composition in travel photography, flipping through the slide deck that illustrated his words.

He was tired. His leg kept him up most of the night, and when he'd finally drifted off to sleep, Maria joined him in his dreams, making him restless. But the room was packed, so he tried to stay focused on his talk, pausing occasionally to meet the eyes of some of the audience.

During one of those pauses, he noticed the woman with the corkscrew curls sitting at the back and taking notes. A plan of sorts formed in his mind. That woman knew Maria, and so he would get to know that woman.

"Excuse me?" A person from the audience had his hand raised. Damn, how long had he been daydreaming?

"Yes?"

"Can you talk more about choosing the best filters for the shot? How do you decide?"

"Great question," said Nathan, turning back toward his slide deck. "I have an example of just that in a moment, and once I get there, if you want to know more, please let me know."

He spoke a half hour more, then answered questions for a few minutes. "Now, here's your assignment," he said. "In two days' time, when we are in Colombia, if you have an opportunity, take a picture of some of the architecture from unusual angles. Send me an example to my email"—he flashed the email address onto the screen— "and I'll critique the first few on our next sea days."

A conference worker came to the door and waved at him, indicating it was time to wrap up. He glanced at his watch, surprised the time had gone by so quickly. "Okay, it's time for lunch, and this afternoon I believe some of you are in the computer room with my son Rory, who can make most pictures look great." Rory stood and waved at everyone while Nathan looked at the schedule. "And here in this room, Belle

McIntyre, aka the Vagabond of the Sea, will be here to talk about how to monetize a blog."

The woman with the corkscrew curls stood and waved at the room, and Nathan smiled. This would be easier than he thought. Belle was the woman Rory had invited to lunch that day. All he had to do was show up.

CHAPTER 9

Maria took her plate of food and walked around the dining area, searching for Belle in their usual places. She found her friend at a table beside the window.

"How was your first session?"

"You would have enjoyed it. It was a photographer who spoke about composition. His pictures were breathtaking. A lot of wildlife but some of architecture and such. He gave us all an assignment to do in Colombia the day after tomorrow. Come with me, and I'll share what I learned."

"It's a date," said Maria. "Anything to improve my photography skills." She had been improving over the years, taking online courses during sea days, and she'd sold a few of her photos to stock companies, which gave her some extra cash.

"You should also start a blog," said Belle.

"The Vagabond's Island Friend?" Maria laughed.

"Why not?" Belle said. "Vancouver Island is a great destination." Then she smiled over Maria's shoulder and waved. "Hi, Rory, we're here."

Maria turned to see who Belle was waving at and froze. A young man approached with a plate of food, while an older man limped behind on crutches.

When they got to the table, Belle introduced them.

"Rory, this is Maria, and this is..."

"Hello, Maria," Nathan said, his dark eyes scrutinizing her face.

"Nathan," she said coolly. "It's been a while."

"You two know each other?" Rory asked.

"Yes," Maria said, standing to leave.

"Maria and I were classmates at high school," said Nathan, continuing to look at her.

"Classmates?" Maria slapped her napkin onto the table. "If that's all we were, Nathan, I'm glad you left. I'm glad you... you..." What was the word she was looking for? "I'm glad you abandoned me."

His brow wrinkled as though he were trying to understand what she was saying.

"What are you talking about?"

She glared at him. "If you don't remember, ask your mother."

Then, remembering that they weren't alone, she turned to Rory and Belle. "It is nice to meet you, Rory. Belle, I seem to have lost my appetite. I'm sorry." She stepped away from the table. "I'll see you at dinner in the dining room."

"I'll come..." Belle started to say.

"No Belle, you stay here and talk photography and blogging. I need some time to myself."

She turned on her heel and walked away toward the gym. She would take a run on the treadmill to get out some of this unexpected anger. Why, after so many years, did his words get to her? He'd made it sound like it had somehow been her fault.

"What was that all about?" she heard Rory ask before she was out of earshot.

"I have no idea," said Nathan, and he had the audacity to sound truly confused.

CHAPTER 10

Nathan leaned heavily on the crutches and watched Maria charge off. Why was she angry with him? She was the one who'd married another man only weeks after he left town. And what did his mother have to do with anything?

"Sit down, Dad," said Rory, placing the plate he had been carrying for his father on the table in front of Nathan. "Eat something. Our next session starts in an hour. I'm going to grab my lunch."

"Right," Nathan said, looking down at his son and the plate of enticing food. He wanted to storm away too, but he was hungry, and he had to eat something, and it would be hard to storm with crutches. He leaned the crutches against the window and sat down next to the empty place Maria had just vacated.

"I'm sorry about that," he said to Belle, who was

watching him with an inscrutable expression.

"So, you're the one," she said.

"*The one?*"

"The one who broke her heart."

"I don't know what's going on here," he said. "But that's not the way I remember it. I came home from three months of training and working in the oil fields to find her married to another man and expecting his child."

Belle opened her mouth to say something, then seemed to think better of it. Instead, she took a sip of coffee and turned to him again. "Nathan, I don't know you, but I know Maria. And the story she told me doesn't match what you're saying."

"I don't understand."

"Maybe you should do what she suggests. Ask your mother if she remembers what happened."

He took a bite of the curried chicken on his plate and chewed for a moment. "My mother is dead."

"I'm sorry. I didn't know. Maybe you just need to wait for Maria to calm down, and you can explain your side of the story. Let her explain hers."

"She's stubborn," said Nathan. "If Maria doesn't want to do something, she won't."

"I'll talk to her."

"Thanks," Nathan said. "I'm not sure it will help,

but thanks for trying." For his part, he would do his own research, starting with Sheila. Maybe she would know what had happened between Maria and their mother.

They ate in silence, and when Rory returned with his own plate, and steered the conversation to blogging, he rose and said, "I'm going to check in with Sheila about Dad before the next session. I'll see you there, Rory?"

Rory nodded and turned back to listen to Belle, who was talking about affiliate marketing and monetizing blogs, a topic Rory was keen on.

Nathan made his way to the room where Rory would teach his first class. He had told his son he would be there to listen, but first he planned to look for pictures to share at his next session on photographing wildlife.

He and Maria had developed a taste for wildlife photography together. They had gone on frequent hikes, looking for birds or small animals to shoot pictures of, and finding places to kiss out of the watchful eye of her overprotective parents. He had continued to learn and practice the craft while he was working in northern Alberta in the oil fields.

A picture of a grizzly bear had jump-started his photography career when he won a contest for a well-known wildlife magazine. He had continued to take pictures and sell them, building up his portfolio as he traveled throughout the north and later took a job in Toronto. When Rory turned eighteen and went out to Emily Carr University to learn graphic design, he left the oil business for good. Three years ago, he had taken a position as a travel photographer alongside a writer, Sanjay, who opened his eyes to new ways of seeing the world. They enjoyed a good partnership for two years before Sanjay got married and began teaching travel writing online. Since then, Nathan had worked freelance—a life he had enjoyed for several months until his recent accident.

He hobbled toward a line of seats at the back of the empty room, swung his laptop bag off his shoulder, and settled into one chair while propping his foot up on another. He pulled out his phone to check his texts and ask Sheila what he wanted to know.

The first text he read was from Jacob: *Dad's stable, and Sheila says she told you and you're working. I'm still pissed you're not coming right away. You always leave me holding the bag.*

Well, at least the battle with his brother was happening over text today. Nathan didn't have the energy to talk to Jake, and communicating this way gave him time to compose a mature response rather than the knee-jerk kind his brother often provoked. Hopefully, by the time he got to Victoria, where his father would travel for surgery, his interactions with his brother would be civil, if not amicable. Thankfully, Sheila was there. He would have to thank her for that. But first he had to know.

Nathan: Sheila, do you remember Maria, the girl I was seeing in high school?

Sheila: Yes, I remember Maria. She got married after high school and moved to Sunshine Bay to be a nurse, I think. Why?

Nathan: Was there anything that went on between her and Mom that you remember?

Sheila: Only the letters.

Nathan: Letters?

Sheila: Maria gave me letters to send to you for a while. I didn't know your address, and Mom said she would send them for me. I always wondered why she stopped writing, but then I found out she was getting married. Why did you break up with her?

Nathan: What makes you think I broke up with her?

He had, but there was something strange about this story. Had Maria written to him? If he had known, perhaps it would have changed the way he went forward in his life.

Sheila: Mom took your last letter to Maria personally. To let her down easy, Mom said.

Nathan: I never wrote any letters.

Sheila: You must have. Mom said…

Nathan: Mom said what?

Sheila: Nate, I don't know what happened. I'm sorry. Mom was… Well, you know how Mom was.

Nathan: Mom was struggling to bring up two kids after her husband left her high and dry.

Sheila: Nate. You weren't here. You don't know. When you come home, let's talk. There are things we never told you about Mom. Things we decided you didn't need to know. You were already doing so much by sending money to me for school and raising a family of your own. We didn't want to burden you.

Nathan: You mean Mom talked to Maria about me?

Sheila: I think so. I don't know. It was such a long time ago. Why are you even dragging it up now?

Nathan: Because Maria is here on the ship, and she just tore a strip off me in the dining room and I don't even know why.

Sheila: You'll have to ask her.

Nathan: I don't think she wants to talk to me.

Sheila: Well, you're on a ship. It's not like she can run very far.

He chuckled.

LOL Thanks Sheila. I'll see you soon.

Sheila: Okay. I'm looking forward to seeing you and Rory. It's been ages since the family was all together.

Nathan: I look forward to seeing you too.

He put his phone back into his pocket and opened his laptop to do some prep work for the next day. After this afternoon's session, he would try to track down Maria—and hopefully they could have a civil conversation.

CHAPTER 11

After Maria stormed off, she headed to the gym and found it full of people, as it always was on the first sea days. So instead, she made her way to the top deck and walked around the ship, breathing in the fresh sea air until she calmed down. When she did, she was embarrassed. She hadn't handled that well at all—but then neither had he, pretending they were nothing to each other. Pretending they had no past.

But maybe he had acted coolly because of his son. If she had been in his shoes, she might have done the same. Though she would have at least called him an old friend. Not a classmate. A *classmate!*

Her ire was rising again, and she tried a meditation technique she had developed over several months.

She stared out into the waves, searching for blow holes. Focusing on the waves helped her calm down, and on a good day, she could see a whale or porpoise in the distance. She breathed in slowly, scanning the sea around her. After ten minutes she had seen no whales, but she felt better.

Turning away from the railing, she started toward the stairs and was run into by a trotting woman wearing a T-shirt that read "Christie's Crones." A pink ribbon held back her salt-and-pepper hair.

"Sorry," said the woman, looking up at her as though Maria would bop her on the nose.

"It was my fault," said Maria, though she didn't really believe it. People shouldn't be running on the deck unless it was on the track upstairs. "I wasn't looking where I was going."

"I was trying to catch up with my friends, though I am not sure why. They are exhausting me."

"Is it a hen party?" she asked, nodding toward the T-shirt.

The woman grimaced. "It's my cousin's third wedding. Finally met the man of her dreams, I suppose. Maybe at fifty-nine she'll finally get it right?"

"Where are you from?"

"I live in Toronto. My cousin's from Victoria. And most of her other 'crones'—she pointed to her shirt

— "are from the island too. They're on their way home."

"Odd woman out?"

She nodded. "I should have just gone to the wedding, but I've always wanted to try a cruise."

"Well, now that you've made the choice, you may as well commit. There's a lot to do on a cruise—everything from line dancing and pickle ball to spending a day in the spa," said Maria.

"I suppose," said the woman. "On the other hand, if you make a decision that doesn't work out, maybe it's time to make a new choice."

"True," said Maria. "Though it's only been a day, and we are on the boat until we dock, so you may as well throw yourself into vacation mode."

The woman laughed. "Yes, I am committed. Thanks for the reminder. Who knows when I'll be this way again?"

Maria smiled at the woman and bade her goodbye just as another woman teetered toward them. Her pink T-shirt read, "Hi, I'm Christie."

"I found you!" she giggled. "Did you get lost again?" She grabbed her cousin's arm. "We're all waiting for you. We're playing blackjack!"

"It was nice talking to you," the woman said over her shoulder as she was pulled away.

Maria waved her off, turned in the opposite direction, and went downstairs in search of a distraction, starting at the library.

She signed out a copy of the next High Seas Book Club selection, took down the details of the first meeting, then sat in a comfortable chair by the window and opened the book.

She leafed through the pages, then read the first page three times without understanding a word. This wasn't helping. She was only avoiding the inevitable meeting with Nathan—and since she had been the one to storm off, she needed to be the one to seek him out. It was the only way to understand what had happened and get some closure.

The conference sessions would be done soon. They were limited to two a day during sea days, which gave people plenty of time to network and practice techniques in the interim. Maria walked down to the meeting rooms, glancing inside each room to see if she could find Nathan.

"Can I help you?" asked a staff member.

"No, I'm just waiting for a friend," she said.

"It'll be another half hour until they break again."

"Thanks." She walked upstairs to deposit her book in her room, then paced for a few minutes to build her courage again. She sat on the bed and looked around at her last stateroom for at least a few months, and her eyes landed on a picture of Evan and Haley.

"Okay," she said to the photograph, "I'm going." She had no choice. As she had told Christie's crone upstairs, once you commit, follow through, no matter how difficult it would be.

She grabbed a cup of coffee on her way back to the meeting rooms so she would have something to hold on to, though coffee made a poor shield, especially after it cooled down. She sat down outside the rooms just as the doors opened and people filed out. She saw Belle and nearly called out to her, but her friend was heavy in an animated conversation with a colleague, and she didn't want to intrude. Belle was in her element, and she was happy for her.

The rest of the people came out of the rooms, and she waited a moment. Had she missed him? She stood and walked into one room, but it was empty. So was the next. Maybe he wasn't here. A reprieve would be welcome, she thought, but so would getting this over with. She turned to enter the last room in the hall when he came out the door, pausing to speak to someone behind him. She walked up to him before she lost her nerve.

"Hello, Nathan. We need to talk."

He staggered a moment. Taken by surprise, she supposed.

"Yes, we do."

Well, that was a start, she thought. She took a deep breath. "Maybe we can find a quiet place? The lounge is usually empty this time of day, and it's close." She glanced at his leg, and he winced.

"Give me a moment." He stepped back into the room to speak to someone, then returned. "Lead the way." His face was impassive but for a tightening of his jaw and those intense eyes boring into hers. This would not be an easy conversation.

"Can I get you a coffee or something?" she asked.

"No. I'm fine. There was water in the conference room."

"Okay, then." She walked ahead—slow enough for him to follow but fast enough that he couldn't see her shaking—and when they got to the empty lounge, she walked toward one of the tables, pulling out a seat for him and waiting for him to settle before taking a seat herself.

"Thanks for coming to find me," he said—just as she said, "I thought we should clear the air."

They looked at each other. "You go first," he said.

"Okay." She paused. "Where do I begin?"

"Maybe you could tell me why you cheated on me with Evan."

She wanted to slap him, but that wouldn't achieve her aim, and she wasn't five years old, so instead she counted to ten in her head, then said, as calmly as she could, "I never cheated on you. Evan and I didn't get together until after you left." How could he accuse her of something like that? Had someone told him that? Rumors had a way of ruining lives. She'd seen that happen before. "I don't know what you heard or who would have told you that, but—"

"You're either lying or your memory is faulty, Maria. It was the week I drove my siblings back to Dad's place in Sunshine Bay. The week after high school was done. That week after you and I finally... Do you remember?"

"How could I forget that? You slept with me after wooing me for more than a year, after making promises of a future together. And then you were gone. How could I forget that?"

"It wasn't like that, and you know it."

"Then what was it like, Nathan? Remind me. Because all I know is that you and I left the graduation party, booked a hotel, and had a night and a morning I will never forget. Then two days later, you left. You went to see your dad and phoned to tell me you didn't want to see me again. Even after that, I wrote you letter after letter. I told you everything that was going on, but you never replied... except by using your mother as the messenger. You used me." She kept her head up as she said it, but was glad she still had the coffee cup in front of her to keep her hands from shaking.

"No. That's not how it happened at all." He shook his head, and she willed herself to stay glued to her seat. To listen. She needed these answers, even if they weren't what she wanted to hear.

"Well, tell me how it went, then. Because that's all I remember."

He sat forward—as best he could with a leg in a cast—and leaned on the table. "When I got home to Victoria, I went to see you."

"You never saw me after the hotel room."

He held up his hand, and she sat back again.

"Okay. Go on."

"It had been a long day. Jake was being the kind of jerk that only thirteen-year-old boys can be. He was angry, picking fights the whole way there, and Sheila was truly irritating because she rolled her eyes at everything he said, and replied 'whatever' to everything. Between the two of them, I was so stressed by the time I got there I felt like pitching them into the sea.

"Then after nearly two hours of that, we got to Dad's, and he barely let me use the bathroom before I was back outside driving home again, leaving them to play Monopoly with Dad's girlfriend and sit around with Dad, joking. They never even saw me leave."

"That must have been difficult," she said. She had sympathy for him. He had told her how hard it had been for his mother when his father left, and she knew about the falling-out between him and his father. But she hadn't thought it was that bad.

"Anyway, when I got home, my grandfather—you remember we moved in with him after my dad left—sat me down to talk. He listened to me rant about my father, and how I figured it was my fault they divorced. Then he waited for me to quit griping and finally said, 'Are you done?'" Nathan chuckled. "I'll never forget the way he had of cutting to the chase."

"I wish I'd known your grandfather, but my father barely let me out of his sight after he found out we were dating."

"I remember. We had to sneak around after that."

"Perhaps it would have turned out differently if we could have been out in the open about things," she mused, and before he could ask what she meant, she said, "Go ahead. You were telling me about what your grandfather said."

"Right, anyway, that's when he told me he was trying to get my mother into rehab and that it was time I found a useful trade where I could work out my anger productively. He had called in a favor and gotten me an interview with a recruiter from an oil company. I could be a rigger. It would be hard work, but they would train me. Then, after a six-month contract, I could decide what I wanted to do next. It was a good opportunity. I had to meet with the guy downtown the next day. The money would be good. My grandfather suggested I go."

Maria rolled that fact around in her brain. Another missing piece to the Nathan puzzle. "I hadn't even known you applied. I think that was the part that surprised me so much, because I never even knew that about you."

"I didn't want to go at first. I wanted to go to college. Make something of myself. But Grandpa had a point. If I managed the money right, I could make enough in six months to cover my college expenses for two or three years. And I was so angry, I had to do something productive."

"But what does any of this have to do with you thinking I was cheating? I never saw you after our night in the hotel. Did someone say something to you?"

He paused again. "After I dropped Sheila and Jake at Dad's place, I came home, and Mom was a mess. When the kids went back to his place, she was always a mess. She was crying, saying how scared she was, that Dad had left her without enough money to support her, that she couldn't find work and had to move home. She went on and on about how she needed to get a house so the kids would have a place to stay, though I knew Dad and the courts would never allow them to stay more than a weekend or two a month—and only then if Grandpa were there. Anyway, I went to the interview to shut her up, and after all the support Grandpa had given me, I felt I owed it to him to at least try. I never dreamed they would hire me. I couldn't turn it down. Not after all that. The money was huge. It was a demanding job, but I could do the work. It also meant giving up college until the following year, but I didn't really know what I wanted to do anyway, so I figured I would go later, once things settled down and I knew what I wanted to do."

"But that doesn't explain why you thought I cheated."

"After I finished the interview, I went to your place

to tell you. To talk to you about it. I was going to see you no matter what your father said." He paused, swallowing.

"And?"

"And I saw you in the backyard with him. You were hugging him close. It was obvious you were together, and I know how you felt about him when you were younger. You told me you had always had a crush on Evan. Besides, he was the kind of man your father would approve of—older, educated, no juvie record."

She stared at him. What was he talking about? She hadn't been with Evan until after. After. Then she realized. "No. No. That's not what happened. I remember that weekend. That was the weekend Evan came home from university. He had just finished a teaching practicum and came home to see his father. It was when—"

"No. I saw you. Together. You were hugging him. Holding him." His face was in anguish.

"*That's* why you phoned and told me you never wanted to see me again? Because I was comforting a friend who had just learned his father was dying?"

"What?"

"Evan had just learned his father was dying from a disease that would take him quickly. And he had just learned that he may have inherited it. It's known as ALS. His grandfather had it. His father had it."

"And he had it?" Nathan searched her face. "Is that why he's not here on the cruise with you?"

"Yes. Evan died three years ago." She choked out the words, willing the tears to stay back.

"I'm sorry."

She waved his words away, blinking hard. "Why didn't you just talk to me, Nathan? I waited for you to come back. I wrote letter after letter. I loved you. I wanted *you*."

"But you married him within two months."

She searched his eyes. They were closed over again, and she realized he must have been so hurt. So angry. He had just lost his family, and then he thought he had lost her, too.

"That's because you never answered my letters."

"I never got any letters," he said.

"That can't be true, Nathan. Why else would you have sent the money?"

"What money?" he looked genuinely confused—which confused Maria in turn. How could he have forgotten what had changed her whole life?

She heard footsteps then, and they both turned.

"There you are," Rory said. "I've been looking all

over for you. They need you up on deck. It's nearly time."

Maria looked between him and his son. They had an easy relationship, a camaraderie. He had been a good parent, it seemed. If he'd stayed, they could have raised children together. But instead, he had left. He hadn't felt she was enough to fight for.

"Right," said Nathan. He turned back to Maria. "I promised I would give the group lighting tips for sunset shots. But I want to catch up more. We need to finish this conversation. After dinner?"

She considered for a moment and then shook her head. She needed time to process what he had told her. "What about tomorrow?"

He looked as though he didn't want to agree, but he relented. "Come by at noon. We can go for lunch."

Then he turned and hobbled away, leaving her with a war of feelings. How could he still be the steady man she had always known? How could he be a good father, a good son, and still have done what he had done? It didn't make sense.

And it especially didn't make sense that, even after all he had done, she felt drawn to him.

She walked toward the elevator to the buffet. She had another two hours before she had to meet Belle in the dining room. Maybe she could find a perfect stranger to have a coffee with, listen to, and get to know, so she could avoid thinking about her own life. Her own losses. It was a tactic that had worked for years now. With Nathan so close, she missed Evan even more than ever. He was the one she had turned to when Nathan left. He had helped her process the loss. And right now, she felt alone.

CHAPTER 12

That night after the demonstration, Nathan joined a group of conference-goers for dinner and answered questions before agreeing to join them at the evening show. The shows were good, they told him, and since this was his first cruise—and the last for a while, if his brother got his way—he agreed.

"You have to throw yourself into the experience," said a woman in the group. "You know, commit." She was looking at him the way women often did. With a certain interest that made him want to put up a shield and run as quickly as possible.

"Dad doesn't commit," Rory said. "He's a lone wolf." That didn't seem to dissuade the woman. It only seemed to pique her interest.

"Thanks, Rory. You make me sound like a poor father."

Rory turned to him, startled. "That's not what I meant."

"Let's go see this show," he said, stopping any further exchange. He wasn't sure what Rory meant, but he didn't want to hear more now.

As they walked to the theater, another woman, who was wearing a T-shirt that said "Christie's Crones" on it, fell into step beside him. He walked beside her for a few minutes, then turned to look at her more closely, avoiding her ample chest.

"It's Nathan, isn't it?" she asked.

"Are you with the conference?" he asked.

"No, I'm with my sister's hen party and I was able to sign up for a few classes after boarding. I'm Bethany and I was up on deck when you were teaching the class."

"Oh! Did you find it helpful?"

"That's why I wanted to talk to you. You're a brilliant teacher. I learned more about lighting from you in a few minutes than I have reading dozens of books. I overheard you saying you would be on the island for a few weeks, and I was wondering if you would consider coming to my photography club and giving a lesson."

"Where are you located?"

"A small town about two hours from Victoria called Sunshine Bay. But we have a big club for a small town."

"I know Sunshine Bay," he said, looking into her hopeful eyes. "Perhaps if the timing works out. I have family down that way I need to visit."

"Oh, that would be wonderful. Maybe I could invite some of the other clubs on the island to join us."

"That sounds like something I would be interested in." He stopped a moment, balanced on one crutch, and fished into his pocket for his card case. He was glad he'd listened to Rory about getting cards made before they embarked. He handed her the card, with one of his bear photos on the front. "We can connect and perhaps set something up for, say, a month from now?"

She took the card and examined it, then turned on a smile that filled the room. This woman needed to smile more often.

"Thank you so much," she said. "I really appreciate this."

"I hope we can work something out. There are more details on the website, and I can give you a conference rate since I'll be on the island anyway."

"Thank you so much," she said again. "I have to

meet my sister and her friends now, but I'll be in touch." She scurried down the hallway the way they had come, leaving Nathan to watch her go.

He grabbed his crutch again and hobbled toward the theatre, glad to find that Rory had saved him an aisle seat at a level that didn't require him to climb stairs in order to escape the woman with the predatory eyes later. He was a good one, his son.

The show was a variety of songs from the fifties, dancing from that era, and a couple of comedy sections to add laughs. Though it wasn't something Nathan would usually go to see, he had to admit it was a fun hour and it left the audience in a good mood.

After the show, he told Rory he was going back to the cabin.

"I'll come too. It's been a long day, and I have the first class in the morning."

When they got to the room, Rory waited until Nathan was settled into the chair before asking the question he had probably been holding in for hours.

"Dad, who is Maria?"

Well, if he wanted to know, he would tell him, and it was time he told him the rest, too.

"Maria was the one who got away, Rory. She was my first love."

"What happened? She said you just left her."

"After talking to her today, I guess that was what I did. But it wasn't quite like that."

Rory sat on the couch and waited for him to elaborate. When Nathan added nothing right away, he said, "Go on. I'm listening."

"I have a question first. What did you mean about me not being able to commit? Was that just to get that woman off my back? Or was there more to it?"

"I don't know why I said that," Rory said. "It was something I heard Mom say often, that's all. It just kind of slipped out."

"Your mother thought I couldn't commit?"

"She told me you were always so wrapped up with your family that you couldn't commit to her. They always seemed to come first. Particularly Grandma."

"Is that what you think?" he whispered. He was finding it hard to catch his breath.

"Dad, you did your best considering your job took you away so much. But I know Mom was lonely. You used to spend so much time dealing with paperwork and things when you were home. Mom said even when you were there, you weren't there. That's why she's so happy with Zane. With you, she always felt second-best. That's what she said, anyway."

Nathan considered that. Ramona had often told him he wasn't there for her, but he had always thought she meant physically, not emotionally. He had to think about this away from his son's prying eyes. Those eyes were so much like his own, and he didn't much like their intensity when they focused on him.

"Want to get a drink?" he asked.

"Dad, you don't drink."

"A decaf latte, then."

"Sure. Let's go. There's a barista in the library."

They walked in silence while Nathan considered what to tell his son. Rory was twenty-one now, and Nathan had worked hard to maintain a relationship with him after he and Ramona separated.

He could tell him the truth, though he wished Trevor were here too. Did Trev think he couldn't commit, either? He and Trevor still had a long way to go to really get to know each other. Though Trevor had been grateful for Nathan's help to start his career, he had always been closest to Ramona, just as Nathan had always been closest to his own mother. Perhaps he should think of settling on the island for a while and making it his home base. But what would he do if he couldn't travel?

When they had settled into two easy chairs in the library, a small table between them for their coffee, he was ready.

"Maria wasn't my first girlfriend, but she was the

one I fell for. Hard. She was my first love, and I thought she was my future."

"But then you left?"

"Actually, it was my dad who left first. Right before I finished high school, he walked out on my mother."

"How did that affect you and Maria?"

"I had to go to work to help my mom. She couldn't make ends meet, and she needed help. Dad got custody and she wanted the kids—Jake and Sheila—to visit, so she needed a safe, stable home. I went to work in the oil fields and helped pay off my grandfather's mortgage. Mom and I lived with him for a few years before he died, and he needed help too. Meanwhile, Maria married another man."

"Man, it would be tough to see her do that."

"Especially since she was married only two months after I left."

"What? Sounds like you were well rid of her. Why would she do that?"

"I don't know, son, but maybe I'll find out more tomorrow. I feel like there is more she wanted to tell me; more I need to know."

Rory nodded, then took a bite of one of the cookies he had brought with the coffee.

"Hey, wait a minute. Is that why you inherited the house after Grandma died? Because you had paid a lot of the mortgage? Trevor says Jake goes on about that all the time. Says you ripped them off by taking the house, that it was worth way more than what he and Sheila got out of her estate. He only got a few thousand. He thinks Grandma liked you best."

"Does he?" Jake had always said that, but Nathan had never known why, especially as he had all their father's love. As far as he could see, Jake was everyone's favorite—the funny little brother who got away with things Nathan would never have tried. He took a sip of his latte, considering what to tell his son so he would understand.

"I didn't inherit the house," he said.

"But you have a house in Victoria that you rent out. I've been there."

"No. The reason I didn't inherit the house was because I bought my grandfather out three years after I left home, and I took over the mortgage. Then I agreed my mom could live there after he died and pay me a small rent—far below market rates, just enough so I could cover the taxes and utilities—so Jake and Sheila would still have a nice place to visit.

"Before Grandpa died, he took most of what he got from the house sale and put it into a trust for Sheila and Jake's education, because though Dad was the more stable of our parents, he didn't have the money for their education fund. The rest we set up in an annualized allowance so Mom would have enough to live on with the money Dad sent. She stayed there until she died. Then I fixed the place up and rented it out to yuppies. Grandpa had bought in a nice neighborhood."

"What did you get from Grandpa's money? Seems like they got way more than you," said Rory.

"Grandpa gave me way more than money. He believed in me. He gave me my first camera. Helped me get my job in the oil fields. And when he died, I got a small amount of money he'd set aside for me to go back to school."

"So why do they think Grandma gave you the house?"

"I don't know. I always thought Dad would have figured out I bought the house, but he probably never told them. He always blamed me for their marriage falling apart."

"Why??"

"I was a difficult teen," said Nathan.

"What? You difficult?"

"Sarcasm Rory? Really?"

"Well, you are kind of frustrating. You never actually tell anyone anything. You are always just away."

Nathan paused."Well, back then, I was angry all

the time. I took my anger out on my dad and he took his out on me. He was always shouting about how much of a disappointment I was, about how I was so much like my mother. And then one day, he just took my brother and sister and left."

"Just like that?"

"My mother had a problem with alcohol, and she wasn't as responsible as she needed to be, so he decided to get the kids away from her influence. "

"And left you behind?"

"I was old enough to leave home."

"How come you never said anything? "

"Because he was probably right. I wasn't a good influence on the kids then. I would have just brought a lot of anger with me. And someone needed to stay with my mom. I couldn't abandon her too."

"So that's why you always run away? "

"I don't run away. I went away to work. I didn't have the education to do anything else that would make the money I was making."

"I know, but I also know that when Mom started dating Zane, you were able to get a job in Toronto. You were able to come home."

"You boys needed me. And until then, I hadn't realized how bad my marriage was. I took your mother for granted, I know that, and Trevor was so angry about Zane, I just needed to try and make something better."

"Yeah, and I think Trevor appreciated it. He and Zane really don't get along."

"Angry teen emotions were something I had experienced," said Nathan. "And I owed it to your mother to let her try to make her new relationship work."

"I never thought of you as an angry teen."

"I've worked hard not to be Rory. It has taken me a very long time."

There was a long silence, and finally Rory picked up his latte and drained the cup. "We should probably go to bed. I'm teaching two classes tomorrow."

"Good idea."

That night, Nathan had a tough time sleeping. His mind raced with thoughts of conversations he'd had with Rory, Maria, and the texts with Sheila. Had he been wrong his whole life about what happened? Did he run away when things got tough?

No. He had left home because his father had rejected him. Maria had rejected him. And he'd deserved it. His father had been right that he would never amount to anything no matter how hard he tried. And he had tried. At least he still had Sheila in his corner. And Rory.

At three o'clock, he was still awake, with a nagging feeling that he was missing something. Something big.

He rolled over on his back, grabbed his phone from the table beside the bed, and sent another message to his sister.

Just wondering if you know anything about what happened to the letters. I never received them.

There was no answer. He didn't really expect one this early in the morning, but a few minutes later an ellipsis appeared on the phone, indicating that she was typing.

We should talk. There are things you should know about when you left home.

Why don't you just tell me

He didn't want to get up and speaking right now would wake Rory.

Sheila: Because it's late, and I need to try to remember the details. Let's just say Mom was convincing when she lied, and I still don't know what was true and what wasn't.

Nathan: Not you too.

Sheila: I know you hate it when we say anything against her, Nate, but you must admit that when you graduated and Dad left, it was a terrible time for her. For us. But most especially for you.

Nathan: I was fine. I just went to work.

Sheila: Can you phone me? Tomorrow morning, I'll be home. I am in the hospital right now.

Nathan: Hospital?

Sheila: Dad had another angina attack. They're going to keep him here overnight.

Nathan: Is he going to be okay?

He had to be okay. His father was always okay.

Sheila: It's just a precaution. I'll let you know as soon as I hear more, but they said it isn't an emergency yet. His surgery is still scheduled for two weeks away.

Nathan: I can call you at ten your time. It will be around noon here.

Sheila: Okay. Talk to you then.

He put the phone back on the table and turned to face the wall again. Why were they always trying to make their mother out to be the bad guy in this? She wasn't the one who'd left them behind and gotten remarried. Sure, she had an addiction, but she wasn't the one who hadn't provided properly for her children. And she wasn't the one who'd abandoned him as soon as he was eighteen.

He closed his eyes and tried to focus on counting backward from one hundred. He got to seventy-two before falling into oblivion.

CHAPTER 13

The next morning, Maria had an early walk on the top deck, grabbed a coffee, then went to the internet café to email her sister. She had been thinking of all the ways she could ask why she had told Haley she was moving home and decided it was best just to be blunt.

Hi Cynthia,

How's Gerrard doing? I hope he is well. I know you must be worried, and I am sorry I haven't been there to help you through.

Not that Cynthia had really been there for her when Evan was sick, she thought. No, Cynthia was too wrapped up in her own life, her own problems. Cynthia was not the person she turned to for anything, because Cynthia was never there. She continued typing out her email.

My next trip was canceled, so I've decided to visit Sunshine Bay for a couple of weeks. I heard that you told Haley I'd visit, and she thinks you told her I was moving home again.

I wish you had spoken to me first, because you've put me in an awkward position. I did not intend to return for good, and I am angry, Cynthia, that you would be so cavalier as to stretch the truth in this way.

There are things going on in my life right now that you know nothing about. I really wish you had asked me. Talked to me. Not made assumptions and then passed them on to others. I want to be clear that I don't want you to do it again. Any communication with Haley about me and my life is for me to make. Not you. I still don't know why you would do that.

Maria

She pressed send before she could think better of it. Cynthia needed to know how angry she was, how much she resented being forced to do something she didn't want to. She didn't want to go back to memories, loneliness, and pity. Nor did she want to give support to her sister while getting nothing in return. And she really didn't want to listen to Cynthia or anyone else go on about Evan and his end-of-life decisions. It was none of their business.

She wanted to go back to bed, hide under the

covers, and wake up to last week in Europe, when everything was fun and carefree. Instead, she would paste on a smile, go to the gym, work out her frustrations, and prepare to meet with Nathan.

CHAPTER 14

Nathan came out of the room after his session and found Maria exactly where she had been the day before. She looked good. Her hair was longer than when they were younger, and streaked with gray, and she was fit, healthy, and vibrant. The kind of woman who turned heads because of the way she walked through life: confident, sure of herself. Today, however, the determined expression on her face made her seem a little intimidating.

Happy that his crutches gave him the excuse to approach slowly, he hobbled up to her, and she rose to meet him.

"Would you like to go to the dining room today?" she asked. "It's not as far to go, and the tables are usually quite private."

"That sounds good," he said hesitantly. She wanted privacy again, which meant yet another difficult conversation. He couldn't wait until tomorrow when all he had to do was take a tour through Cartagena, Colombia, show people how to form a good composition, and return to the boat for dinner, a show, and a well-deserved rest.

She led the way, and he followed, appreciating how she moved gracefully past the people in the corridor but at a pace he could keep up with.

The maître d' seated them in a booth away from the front of the room, and they settled in to review the menu. She recommended the crab cakes and salad and he agreed, but when she asked if he wanted a glass of wine, he declined. When she was out of questions about food, and after the server had taken their order, he asked, "Shall we continue from where we left off?"

"Uh, sure." She smiled at the server, who returned to the table with a glass of white wine for her and a glass of water for him.

"You said that my mother came to see you. To bring you money. What was that about?" He watched her face, and she looked angry, confused. Was she trying to come up with a lie?

She took a sip of wine. "I wrote you letters. About

six, if I remember correctly. Sheila, your sister, was working for the summer at the same restaurant where I was working, remember? I helped her get the job?"

He had forgotten that, but she was right. She had helped Sheila, fifteen at the time, get her first job. "Yes, I remember."

"Anyway, you never gave me your address, so Sheila said she would ask your mother to put my letters in with hers when she sent them. She told me your mom sent letters once a week and always included one from her and one from Jake when he wrote them."

That was true. He got a letter through the company once a week and always enjoyed hearing from his mother and siblings. "I received no letters from you, Maria."

"But you must have. Otherwise, why did you send the money?"

"What money?"

"After I sent the letter telling you I was pregnant, your mom came to see me and told me you had sent money to help me get rid of the problem."

He stared at her, not comprehending what she was saying, then shook his head. "I don't know what you're talking about. Are you saying you were pregnant?"

"Yes. It seems the precautions we took weren't effective that night."

He thought back to that night, as he had many times in the past thirty-three years. He'd always wondered how she could fake that passion. He tried to remember the details. Condoms. They had used condoms. Most of the time. They'd had intercourse a few times that night. Did they use condoms every time? He couldn't remember, but if what she was saying was true, it didn't matter now. She had become pregnant, and he had left her alone.

"I never knew," he said, feeling as though he'd been sucker punched. "I never got any letters, and I never knew you were pregnant. And if I had, I would never have sent someone to give you money. What do you take me for?"

But he could tell by the look on her face what she thought. She thought he was lying. Thought he was a jerk. A monster. No wonder she had wanted to marry someone else. Why would his mother have done this? Because based on Maria's account and what Sheila said, his mother had not sent the letters they had entrusted to her. In fact, she must have read them herself and acted on what she'd discovered or else why would she have offered Maria money? He wished he could ask her why.

"I didn't know what to do," she said. "I was eighteen and pregnant. I was supposed to be going to university to become a nurse, and my parents... Well, you remember how strict they were. They would have killed me, or at least disowned me, if they'd known. I was terrified."

"What did you do?"

"I turned to the only person I thought I could trust."

"Evan."

This was his fault. He had left her pregnant and alone, had driven her into the arms of another man and run away. He should have just talked to her. Trusted her.

She nodded. "Evan had already confided in me something he didn't really want to share with others, so I felt safe telling him. He said he would help me."

"I should have been there." He reached out and grasped her hand. "Please forgive me."

She slipped her hands out of his grasp and leaned away from the table, picking up the wineglass. He noticed her hands were shaking. It was undoubtedly difficult to relive.

"Let me say the rest, okay? I need to tell you what happened, so you understand why I did what I did."

"I left you alone and vulnerable. I understand why you had to end the pregnancy."

"But that's just it, Nathan. Evan and I got married. He could never have children of his own because of his condition, so I had the baby. We raised her together. "

He swallowed, staring at her in disbelief.

"Haley is a lovely young woman. She's smart, caring, and I am so very proud of her."

"I have a daughter?"

"Yes. She's a nurse. She lives in Toronto with her fiancé, Lance, who has been studying to be an oncologist."

"I have a daughter? Why didn't you tell me before now?"

"Weren't you listening?"

"Right. Yes. You thought I knew. You thought I had asked you to procure an abortion. What must you have thought of me?"

"Let's just say it wasn't always flattering." She smiled at him and then at the server, who was coming to the table with their meals. "Thank you," she said as he placed the plates in front of them. "It looks good."

"Does she know about me?" Nathan asked once the server left.

"Yes. We told her Evan wasn't her father when he

started to get symptoms of ALS. We didn't want her to worry that she would inherit it."

"How did that go?"

"She was angry at first. Mostly at me. But a lot of that had to do with grief, I think. She loved Evan. He was the best of fathers. Kind, present, supportive. Not like my dad, who was distant even when he was home."

Not like me, Nathan thought. Away all the time. Though he had been there for his boys as much as he could, given the circumstances.

"And how is it now?"

"It's been four years since we told her. Three since Evan died. And the last time I visited with her at Christmas—we spent it in Germany—we had a wonderful time. Reconnected. I think she has forgiven me. Mostly, anyway. She'll be in Victoria when we land, and I'm looking forward to seeing her."

"I guess her coming to see you on the island is a good sign."

"She isn't coming to see me. That's just a fortunate coincidence," she said. "She and her fiancé are moving to Victoria. He landed a position in the oncology department at the hospital, and she's got a job as a community health nurse. They are going to be there permanently."

"Would she meet me?" A daughter. He had a daughter! He had always wanted a daughter.

She took a bite of food and chewed for what took ages. He waited. Holding his breath. Finally, she swallowed, took a sip of water, put down her fork, and looked at him.

"Yes. I promised her I would introduce you if I ever found you again. It was one thing I had been intending to do when I went home." She picked up the fork again and concentrated on stabbing a cherry tomato.

"Is that why you've avoided going home for three years? You wanted to keep me out of her life forever?" Anger flared in him. Then he remembered how it had looked to her, and he talked himself down. *Be grateful you know now.*

She stared at him a moment, the skewered tomato hovering near her plump lips. Those lips parted enough for the fork to enter, then closed around the fork before she chewed slowly again. He shifted in his chair, his pants suddenly tighter.

Her gaze continued to focus on him as she chewed, and he waited, wanting to shake her.

Or kiss her.

Finally, she put the fork down again. "I hadn't considered that before," she said. "Maybe that was one reason why I was avoiding home. But that wasn't the main reason."

"What was the main reason?"

"I didn't want to remember what I had lost. And I promised Evan I would live my life as fully as possible. Go on adventures. Refuse to settle. Going home felt like failing, like I would be doing what was expected of me."

"And are you happy in this nomadic life? "

"I thought I was. Yes. It's been interesting. But things are changing."

"Your daughter is coming back."

"That, and my sister's husband isn't well, and Belle, who I have traveled with for two years, is thinking of finding a place to settle on land. Then there's the minor matter of my next trip being canceled because of that collision last week."

"So, a perfect storm."

She laughed. "I suppose you could say that."

"I know how you feel. I've also been traveling for a few years. Travel photography has become my second career. But now I'm struggling with my foot, my father is about to have open-heart surgery, and my sons want to settle on the island. They want me to join them."

"Sons? You have more than just Rory?"

"Trevor, my oldest, is twenty-three. He's working in Sunshine Bay for my brother, Jake."

"Oh! I remember Jake. He was a cute kid. He used to tag along with you when he was little. He looked up to you so much."

"Did he?" Nate couldn't remember a time when Jake ever thought anything positive about him. But perhaps it was true. He was quickly learning that he remembered things differently than others. Sheila had said as much. Sheila. Damn, he was supposed to phone her. How could he have forgotten? He sent her a quick message that he would call her soon.

"Do you have to call someone?" She was looking at him with amusement, her grey eyes sparkling. "Or are you going to show me a picture of your son?"

"I forgot to call Sheila. I need an update about how my father is doing."

Her face became serious. "Go ahead, then. I can take a walk if you need privacy."

"No, I'll just send her a quick text. Let her know I'll call her in about an hour." He keyed in the message quickly then put down the phone. "Speaking of pictures..."

She bit her lip. "I thought you would like to see some." She held out her phone to show him a picture of Haley. "Here's one of Haley I took at

Christmas, here's one of her and Lance, and here is one that was taken about a month ago when she was out hiking, I think." She turned the phone toward her and looked to make sure. "She sends me pictures whenever she does something new, and I send her mine." She turned the phone around again to show him more but lost her place. "Just a minute." She got out of her seat and slid into his side of the booth so the phone was between them. He swallowed hard as he watched her scroll through several more shots. She smelled so good. Like sunshine and the tropics. He wondered what kind of shampoo she used. Whatever it was, it was making it hard for him to concentrate.

When she got to the last picture, a close-up, he put his hand over hers to bring the phone closer, ignoring that she tensed her muscles at his touch. He focused on this image of a woman he had never met but who was rapidly becoming one of the most important women in his life. "She's beautiful, Maria. She looks just like you."

"She has your eyes, though," she said.

"Yes, she does." He wasn't sure how he felt about having two children with his eyes, especially if they focused on him. Maria had once told him his eyes made her feel exposed. As though he could see right inside her, know her secrets. Rory sometimes made him feel that way.

"Here." She extricated her hand from his grasp and cleared her throat. "I have a couple more that were taken in France two years ago." She scrolled through the hundreds of pictures on her phone—the Acropolis, the Eiffel Tower, Florence, and London—until she got to two pictures of her and Haley frolicking in the sand in bathing suits. He looked closely at the pictures, then wished he hadn't. Maria looked good in that suit. Looking at pictures and having her so close was dragging up memories, feelings, longings. He swallowed, then licked his lips. She was going to have to leave before he could stand in public.

"These are great," he said, handing her the phone and looking up at the approaching server.

"Can I get you any dessert?" the server asked, placing their coffee in front of them. Maria turned her head to look at him, a question in her eyes. Or was it a promise?

"No, thank you," he said to the server. "I think we have everything we need."

Maria poured a little cream into her coffee and stirred it. Not moving. Still close to him on his side of the booth. Perhaps he should have shifted away to put space between them, but he didn't want to. He wanted to lean closer and breathe in more of the lavender scent from her hair.

She drank some of the coffee and then put down her cup. "I have some more pictures on the computer in my room, from when she was a baby all the way up to graduation. Would you like to see them?"

"I would. I would also like to meet her. Talk to her. Do you think we could arrange a call?"

"Probably. I would need to call her first, let her know I've found you. Prepare her a bit. But, yes, I think she would like that."

"Thank you. And thank you for telling me. I know it must have been difficult. "

"It was easier after I met Rory. He is a nice young man. You and his mother must be proud."

"We are, but we aren't together anymore. His mother lives in Seattle with her new husband. We separated when the boys were in their late teens."

"And you?"

"I'm on my own. It's hard to have a partner when you travel all the time.'

"Yes, that's true," she said, taking another sip of coffee, and still not moving. "Do you want to come to my room to see the pictures?"

"Uh-huh."

"Would now work?"

He nodded, then remembered both his sister and his physical discomfort. “Actually, can I maybe catch up with you later? I should call Sheila.” *And get away from you so I can get some perspective.* Because what he wanted to do was follow her to her room and right into her bed.

She looked disappointed but quickly smiled. “Of course. I’ll be hanging around with Belle tonight, probably. I’m sure we will run into each other.”

He watched her leave, then took a big gulp of coffee, scanned his phone for urgent messages, and sent another text to Sheila asking for another half hour’s grace. He would go to the room to talk to her. See if she could help him understand why his mother had done what she so obviously had done.

Ah, cruise life is busy. All that eating and drinking. She answered with an *LOL* at the end then typed, *No change, Dad’s still fine. Talk to you soon.*

He sent her a quick waving emoji back, slid carefully out of the booth, and hobbled to the door.

CHAPTER 15

Maria slunk toward her room, feeling like a woman who'd brought a cue stick to a pool party. She was on the back foot and feeling stupid. Mortified!

Why had she flirted with him? How could she get the signals all wrong like that? What must he think of her? She was sure she had felt a connection—that old connection they'd had so long ago. But she'd been wrong. All he wanted from her was information about his daughter. About the letters he said he hadn't received.

Did she believe him? Maybe. He'd looked genuinely stunned when she told him she'd been pregnant. And he looked happy to find out he had a daughter. And when he'd seen her picture, he even seemed to think she was still beautiful.

He'd even said it, for heaven's sake. She hadn't imagined that. Nor had she imagined the tension between them, but it may have been from a different cause than she imagined. Maybe she'd read him wrong.

Knowing that he hadn't left her pregnant, that he'd genuinely thought she'd been cheating on him like his father had done to his mother, she had felt all the old animosity evaporate. In its place, all the old feelings had returned. The attraction, the naked need, the... love?

But he obviously didn't feel that way anymore. Too many years had passed. Too many things had changed. She needed to face facts. Her feelings for him were only a fantasy based on a long-past relationship between teenagers and now even their children were way past their teens.

She had to push this to the back of her mind and help Nathan and Haley build a relationship. Haley deserved to know her father. And Nathan deserved... oh no. She had forgotten to tell him he was going to be a grandfather.

She would call Haley first. A rediscovered father and two half-brothers would be a lot of information for her to handle. This was about Haley and Nathan.

She was just the catalyst that would bring them together.

CHAPTER 16

Nathan walked to his room and collapsed onto the bed. After spending a restless night, teaching a class, and then discovering he was a father again, all he wanted to do was take a nap. He closed his eyes a moment, but all he could see was Maria sitting across the table from him, Maria sitting beside him in the booth, Maria looking at him as though she thought he would be a good dessert.

What had he been thinking, begging off like that? He was sure he'd read the signs that she was attracted to him. But he needed to get perspective first. He needed to find out all he could about his mother because it didn't seem right that he had a daughter he'd never known about. And it didn't seem right that his mother would have kept it from him.

But if that were the case, what else had she kept from him? What else in his life had been built on lies and deception?

He pulled out his phone and called Sheila.

"Well, hello there," she said after only one ring. "You finally found some time in your busy schedule to call, did you?"

"You know how it is," he said. "Hard to squeeze in a call in between breakfast, brunch, lunch, tea, and dinner." He rubbed his stomach which was still far too full.

She laughed. "Well, at least Rory won't starve on this trip. That boy can pack away a ton of food."

"True. Though it isn't nearly as bad as it was a couple years ago. He looks quite different from the last time you saw him."

"Natalie has grown, too. She's fifteen now, you know."

"Really? She was tiny last time I was there."

"That's because you need to visit more often."

"Yes, and now I have more reasons to do that," he said. "Sheila, I have to ask you something."

"Sure."

"When you said Mom lied a lot. What did you mean?" Nathan edged his foot up onto a pillow and tried to get more comfortable.

She sighed. "I knew you wouldn't let that go. And I don't like to speak ill of the dead. She was our mother, after all..."

"But?"

"Mom was a drinker."

"I know she was a drinker, but Dad was too."

"No, Nate. Dad stopped drinking so much after he left—but her problem got worse. Jake and I didn't tell you. You had enough to worry about with your own family, and we knew you bailed Mom out sometimes."

"What didn't you tell me? And why?"

"Mom could be mean, and it was always about the next drink. That's why Jake wanted to live with Dad, and I spent as much time in Sunshine Bay as I could—until Dad started living with Felicia. She was horrible."

"I didn't know it was that bad. Mom drank some when I was younger, but I always thought Dad drove her to it with his affairs."

"That probably didn't help, but it was more about her childhood, I think. Mom didn't have a great time growing up. She told me some stories about Grandma I will never repeat. But I'm still glad I didn't live with her for long. She was always angry, always paranoid, always assuming I'd done something or was trying to keep things from her."

"I wish you'd told me." Nathan stared up at a towel monkey hanging from a clothes-hanger. The cabin crew had been creative today with the linen.

"I tried, but you loved her and would never hear a bad thing about her."

Had he done that? Not listened to what they were saying? Possibly. He had been pretty self-absorbed when he was in his twenties.

"I'm sorry I didn't listen. I guess I was just trying to make things work, and I figured you were both on Dad's side."

"There weren't any sides. Just a broken marriage. But she had secrets. I have no idea where she got the money for the house or for my education or Jake's. We assume she must have had a sugar daddy. Or worse."

Well, he could at least put their minds at rest on that score.

"Sheila, I paid for the house."

"What?"

"I bought Grandpa out of the house, and I paid for the utilities directly. When Grandpa died, I set her up on an allowance. But the allowance wasn't enough to pay for a habit like that."

"But..." There was a long silence. "You paid for our school too, didn't you?"

“Yeah. I paid for that, and for her life insurance policy so you would have an inheritance.”

“Oh, my… I should have figured this out years ago.”

“But there’s something I don’t understand,” said Nathan.

“What?”

“Why do you think Mom wouldn’t have told me Maria was pregnant?”

“Maria was pregnant?”

“Maria was pregnant when she got married. With my baby. She says she wrote me letters, but I never got any letters. Then Mom gave her money and said I had sent it to help her get rid of the problem.”

“Oh Nathan, I am so sorry. I didn’t know. But Mom did things like that. She lied. She even passed off a bad check once for five hundred dollars and phoned me to cover it. Then, when I refused to cover anything more, she moved on to Jake. He told her if she did it again, he’d call the police himself. All I can think is that she had an illness, Nate. She was an addict. She did her best by us, I think, but after Dad left and stopped protecting her, she just fell apart. Maybe she thought she’d lose you too if you had a baby.”

That rang true. She had lost a lot, and his mother was probably desperate. “Maria didn’t follow through," he said. "I have a daughter, Sheila." He loved the feeling of those words on his tongue.

"A daughter! Oh Nate. I wish I'd known. Mom told me you were dating other girls, that Maria had just been a crush. That you asked me not to pass any more of her letters to you. Nathan. If I'd known, I would have told you."

"Well, hopefully there are no more secrets where she is concerned." There was no use being angry with his mother. He would never know why she did what she did. "We just have to move on from here."

"What's her name? Your daughter?" asked Sheila.

"Haley. Her name is Haley. And she's beautiful, just like her mother."

"So that's how it is," said Sheila.

"What?"

"You still have feelings for Maria." Sheila laughed and Nathan pictured her teasing him about kissing Maria one day when she had caught them together in the alley behind the restaurant where they were working.

"Not sure about that. It's been a long time," said Nathan.

"Yeah, sure. If you say so." He could tell by the tone in her voice that she didn't believe him. "I hope we get to meet Haley."

"I hope so too." Nate thought again of Haley 's pictures. She seemed to have a good life, his daughter. She had traveled, finished school, was working in a job she enjoyed. Would she be like that if he had raised her? He would never know, but he would make up for lost time as best he could. He owed her that. "Right now, I'm just going to take it one day at a time."

"Sounds like a sensible plan," said Sheila. There was a pause on the line and then she continued. "Nate, I'm sorry we didn't tell you what was going on."

"Forget it," said Nate. "We'll just have to learn to communicate better now. I had no idea she never told you about the house, either."

'No. But don't hate her, Nate. She couldn't help it. She had an addiction. She was ill. She loved us as best she could."

"I don't hate her. She and Grandpa took my side when I got arrested that time. They believed in me. Unlike Dad. "

"Dad made a mistake. I think he knows that now. He's just stubborn."

"He hasn't spoken to me in years."

"I know, but he told me once that he waited until you were out of detention before he left. That he knew our grandfather would help you as best he could. We were young enough to go with him, and you were old enough to be on your own soon. But he couldn't stay any longer. It was just too much for him. She was too much."

"Sheila," Nathan thought about how to say this so his sister would understand. "Listen, I know that's probably what he told you, but he abandoned me. He didn't believe that I hadn't stolen that car. He let me blame myself for their divorce. I'm not his son. He didn't want me."

"That's ridiculous. You look just like him."

"Mom said my father is someone else."

"So you wouldn't leave her too," said Sheila. "That's how desperate she was to not be left alone."

"Maybe she lied, but he could have reached out anytime in the last thirty years, and he didn't. The ball is in his court, Sheila."

"Maybe, but you know how proud he is."

"Listen, I don't want to talk about him. He's had his chance to apologize and make things right, but he can't, or won't. I just wish I'd known about Mom and the letters years ago. I would have made different choices."

"But then you wouldn't have those wonderful boys of yours."

"Maybe," he said. "But I could have saved Ramona a lot of grief. I never gave her what she needed. She said I had commitment issues. Perhaps I still do."

"Or perhaps you had already committed to someone else and had your heart broken," said Sheila. "Like I did."

Nathan wrinkled his brow, considering what Sheila was saying. Was that why he couldn't commit to another woman? Because he had already fallen for Maria?

"You there, Nate?"

"Yeah, I'm here."

"I know you and Dad have had your issues, but he's been asking for you. Keep an open mind when you get here, okay? If not for yourself or him, then for Jake. He doesn't understand what happened, and when I tell him, he doesn't want to listen. He just blames you for leaving."

"Dad kicked me out."

"I know that now. But we didn't know for a long time. Grandpa told me what happened, but not until years later. I know you don't have to come, but I'm hoping you will."

"I'll think about it, Sheila. I'll be there in two weeks. Meanwhile, thanks for holding things together there and for keeping me up to date on his condition."

"Jake doesn't know everything. Dad would never let me tell him. That's why he's so angry."

"I know."

"Maybe if you let me tell him you've been helping all along, he'll understand."

"Maybe. Or he'll find another reason to be angry. Jake needs to be angry about something."

"That's the plight of being a Stein," said Sheila. "We've all had reason to be angry."

Nathan laughed. "Yes, I suppose we have. I'll see you soon."

They ended the call, and Nathan dropped the phone on the bed beside him, unable to find the energy to get up. Why hadn't he known his mother was passing bad cheques? What else hadn't they told him?

He thought again about what Sheila had said and realized she was right. No woman he brought into his life would ever be enough. And it wasn't their fault. Because he didn't have commitment issues. He had committed his heart years earlier. To Maria. The love of his life.

CHAPTER 17

Maria stayed in that evening, avoiding the crowds and taking the time to consider her options. She should probably call her sister and apologize for the curt email, and she had to phone Haley to tell her about Nate.

But both could wait.

She still needed to decide what to do next. Not what she *had* to do, because as Evan used to say, you could spend your whole life fulfilling other people's expectations and never really live. To honor herself and her needs, she needed to decide what she really *wanted* to do. She was at a crossroads, just as she had been the day Evan had left her, and she had to decide which way to go next.

She brought a cup of tea and dinner out onto the balcony, along with a pad of paper and pen. It was time for the pros and the cons of continuing her life as a vagabond versus going ashore. Though she knew in her heart what she was going to do, she owed it to herself to examine the situation. To make sure it all worked out on paper. She drew a line down the center of the first page.

On the plus side, she still had so many more places to see—though, on the minus side, she wasn't sure this was the way she wanted to travel in the future. Cruising allowed you to see life only around the edges of continents, and she wanted a different type of adventure, like when Haley had gone off to university and she and Evan had backpacked through Spain. It was a slower means of travel, but you experienced more of the local life and could take time to stop if you wanted to rather than be tied to the ship's itinerary.

On the plus side, cruising meant she wouldn't have to put up with the day-to-day problems her sister shared. On the minus side, she missed speaking to Cynthia on a regular basis, and missed hearing about her children, her hobbies, her projects. She could always count on Cynthia to have a project on the go.

On the plus side, she didn't have to cook. On the minus side, she had always enjoyed cooking. She missed family gatherings, missed having friends over, entertaining, and wanted to try some recipes in the few books she had gathered during her travels.

On the plus side, there were so many people to meet while traveling, so many things to learn. She had made friends from all over the world, and she still communicated with them through Facebook, but unless she met another companion like Belle, any in-person relationships she created ended when the ship docked. And those virtual relationships she had created were just as easily maintained on land.

Finally, on the plus side, traveling solo on a cruise ship meant she could do whatever she wanted, whenever she wanted. There would be no one to hem her in. No one to expect anything from her. On the minus side, she was alone—and could be lonely. And she would miss seeing her grandchild grow up.

She sat back and looked at the list, content with her decision to return home. She needed to be a more constant part of Haley 's life again. But with this decision came a whole new set of things to think about.

Would she return to the house she had built with Evan, the one where Haley had grown up? The one that was, if she were honest, just too big for her now? Or should she sell and move to a condo in Victoria? She had certainly adapted to living with very little in the past three years. A condo by the ocean, perhaps.

So she could still look out and see the water every morning. Maybe she could even sit out on a deck as she did here, watching the seagulls frolic and dreaming of where she might go next. Just because she returned to land didn't mean she couldn't travel again.

She looked at her watch and saw that it was only eight. If she called Haley now, she could catch her before she settled in for the evening.

"Hi, Mom, what's up?"

"I have something I need to tell you."

"What? Aunt Cynthia said you had something personal going on."

"When did you speak to Cynthia?"

"About an hour ago. She's worried. She said you were mad at her for telling me you were moving home and asked me if I knew what was wrong with you. You aren't sick, are you?"

Bloody Cynthia. The woman couldn't hold her tongue for a second. Now she was worrying Haley unnecessarily, just three years after Haley had lost her father.

"That's what I need to tell you about."

"Is everything okay?"

"Um. Yes. I mean no, I'm not sick. It's not that."

"Well, you might as well just say it, then."

"I ran into a man on the ship."

"You mean you have a new man in your life? Is that why you may not move back to the island?"

"Actually, he's an old man. I mean, he was in my life a long time ago. Haley, Nathan Stein, your biological father, is here. On the ship. I just spoke to him. He knows about you. We've aired our differences. We both understand what happened. Why things went the way they did."

"And?"

"And he would like to meet you, of course. But also, he has two sons, Rory and Trevor, so you are a big sister with two half-brothers. One is on the ship with him. The other is an apprentice mechanic working in Sunshine Bay."

"Wow," said Haley. "I wasn't expecting that. I kind of thought you didn't want me to meet him."

"I didn't. I wasn't sure how to tell him. I was told he wanted nothing to do with you, but I was deliberately misinformed. Lied to. I know that now, and I am so glad that he wants to meet you. I've seen him with his son, and I think he's a good father, just like your dad was. I think you would like him. So, when we dock, I thought maybe we could all go for lunch, and you can say hello. Then, if you want to know him more, we can arrange it."

"But what happened?"

"It's complicated. I want to explain it to you in person. But meanwhile, you can look forward to meeting him."

"Can you send me a picture?"

"I'll ask him for one of him and his boys. He's a photographer."

"I have so many questions."

"Well, maybe write them down, and I'll see if I can get him to answer some while we're on the ship. He'd like that too, I think." And it would give Maria and Nathan a project to work on together to get past the awkwardness of that afternoon.

"Mom, I know this must be hard for you, reconnecting with a man who left you alone and pregnant, but I appreciate it. And could you please email Aunt Cynthia and see how she's doing? She's going to drive me out of my mind."

Maria laughed. "Okay. I will. And maybe let me tell her about Nathan. Cynthia doesn't know Evan wasn't your biological father. You are the only person we ever told because you are the only person who needed to know."

"You never told your sister?"

"No. She was sixteen at the time, and my parents forbade me. Then I promised your father I wouldn't tell anyone until he was gone. We just kept it to ourselves. Besides, Cynthia can't keep a secret. It would have nagged at her like a badger in a cage until she had to let it out."

"After my conversation with her today, I can see why you wouldn't share that with her. Is it true you aren't going to return to Sunshine Bay to live?"

"I haven't decided yet. I will return to the island, but I might settle closer to where you're going to live. There's more to do in Victoria. Maybe I can get a job there. I could work in a clinic or retrain and take a specialty. I just can't return to hospital work. Not after your dad's illness. It would just be too hard. Besides, I don't want to work full-time. But I could work part-time again."

"Really, Mom? I've missed you."

"Just don't tell Cynthia. She'll be horrified when I tell her I might like to live somewhere else. I may need to break it to her gently."

"Don't worry, I can keep the badger in the cage."

Maria chuckled. "I'll talk to you soon. If I can arrange it, maybe I can set up a call between you and Nathan in the next few days."

"I'd like that."

"Love you, sweetheart."

"I love you too, Mom."

She ended the call with a smile on her face. That

had gone better than expected, but she was sure glad she'd never told Cynthia about Nathan. That would have been all over town before Haley was even born.

THE NEXT MORNING, the ship arrived in Cartagena, and Maria met Belle at the ship's theatre to wait to join their excursion: a walking tour of the walled city.

"So, what's going on with you? I haven't talked to you in over twenty-four hours," said Belle.

"Nothing, really, just working things through with Nathan, telling my daughter about her father, and figuring out my next move once the ship docks."

"So not much, then," Belle deadpanned. "No, seriously, tell me everything."

Maria gave Belle a recap of her conversation with Nathan.

"He's her father? And he didn't know?"

"No. He left town before I could tell him and never returned my letters. Then I married Evan a month later and put him behind me."

"That was pretty quick."

"My parents were so ashamed that I was pregnant. They rejected me. Evan always wanted children, and we had known each other forever, and truth be told, I always had a soft spot for him."

"So, you married to make your parents happy?"

"I was eighteen. Terrified. I did what they asked and never told anyone. My sister doesn't even know. But then, when Evan was diagnosed, he said we had to tell Haley. She's a nurse and would have worried she would inherit the gene."

"How did she take it?"

"She was so angry with me. So angry we hadn't told her. But after so many years, I rarely thought about Nathan."

"Until the other day," said Belle.

"Yes. And now he knows, and she wants to meet him, so I'm going to help make that happen."

"How do you feel about it?"

"Well, so far, I think he's a good man. He seems like he's grown up. Not the angry hot head I once knew. And he's good with his son."

"He does seem like a good father. And he's kind of hot, too."

"You really are a pain," laughed Maria. "Let's talk about something else, okay? Have you been enjoying the conference?"

Their numbers were called then, and they rose to follow the guide's instructions.

"I have. I took Nathan's workshop yesterday morning. He's great at explaining things. He should have been a teacher."

"He's always had patience. Comes from having younger siblings, I suppose."

"He's divorced, you know. Ex is already remarried." Belle waggled her eyebrows, and Maria laughed.

"I knew that, yes." She stayed carefully neutral, wishing Belle would drop the subject.

"And his son seems to think you've caught his eye."

Maria thought about her failed flirtations from the day before and shook her head. "I don't think so. He's only interested in me because I'm the mother of his daughter."

"And why are you blushing at the mere mention of his name?"

"I'm not blushing," she said, knowing that the heat in her face had just heightened.

"If you say so."

"I do," said Maria, and she stepped ahead of Belle in line so she could avoid eye contact until her face cooled again.

The day was warm and humid when they stepped off the tour bus in the heart of the walled city and followed the guide through the cobbled streets, admiring the centuries-old colonial buildings.

At the end of the tour, they were left to their own devices at the market, a goldenrod-colored building filled with stores selling trinkets, souvenirs, and clothing.

Belle and Maria practiced shots using some techniques Belle had learned, and they wandered through the stores, staying a little longer in the ones with electric fans to relieve the stickiness of the day.

“I can’t wait to look at these on the computer,” said Belle as she looked at her camera. “Rory knows how to use software to enhance the shots even more. I’m really looking forward to that class. It’s the day after tomorrow.”

“Tomorrow should be fantastic,” said Maria. “I’m really looking forward to going through the canal. I’ve done some reading about how they made it. Can you imagine cutting through the bush, much less the land? And without modern equipment?”

“I’ve never gone through locks on a ship before, though I’ve seen them in action in Ottawa. But the canals there are a heck of a lot smaller than this one.”

“I saw them use one in Georgetown when Evan and I traveled through the States one year. They were older but operated on the same principle.”

“Tomorrow it will take several hours, so I’m hoping to get some great shots for my blog.”

They walked to the end of the street and watched the other cruise passengers rush in and out of the stores. "There's nothing I really want to get. Let's wait outside for the bus. Maybe we can take some shots of birds while we wait."

"I don't think I'll miss the cruise ship life, but I might miss this." Maria waved at the sight in front of her. "I've enjoyed waking up in a new city every few days, seeing the sights, trying the food."

"You've decided to go home."

"Yes. Now that I'm going to be a grandmother, I think I'd like to."

"You don't look old enough to be a grandmother, Maria," a voice said from behind them. They turned to see a man stepping off a scooter.

"Rory!" said Belle. "How are you enjoying the sights?"

"This is great. I just wish I had more time to wander around the country. I love the lush greenery, the bright colors. I'm getting some great shots of the doors and facades on the buildings."

"I thought you'd like Central America," said Belle.

"What's this about you being a grandmother? I didn't even know you had kids," said Rory.

Maria wasn't sure what to say. Hadn't Nathan told him about Haley? Maybe he didn't want anyone to know. She would have to ask him about it—not jump to conclusions like Cynthia did.

"I have a daughter. She's living in Ontario, and she just told me she's getting married and going to have a baby."

"Well, that's great news. I think my dad would love a grandchild. He's like a magnet for two-year-olds. They seem to adore him, but I'm waiting for Trevor to take that on. I've got too many places to go, things to see, people to meet, to settle down."

"You've caught the travel bug from your father, have you?" asked Maria.

"I guess so, yeah. Dad's been traveling my whole life. He's been everywhere. Have you ever seen his photographs?"

"I've seen a few, yes," said Maria, not wanting to tell him she'd googled his website the night before. What she had found was breathtaking. She wished she had half his talent.

"Get him to show you the ones from his trip to South Africa. That was his last trip."

"Perhaps I will. Where is your father? Did he stay on the ship?"

"What? No. Dad wouldn't let a little thing like multiple fractures slow him down. He took a hop-on-hop-off tour and is traveling with a few of the people from the conference. Giving them tips. Seeing the sights. It's not his usual speed, but he'll enjoy it. Dad always enjoys traveling. It's too bad he won't be able to do it like he used to."

Maria wanted to ask why, but before she could, Rory was talking again.

"Listen, I'm going to return this scooter, so I have plenty of time to get back on board. I'll see you on the ship? Want to have dinner?" He was talking to Belle now.

"There's a barbecue on deck tonight. How about we meet there at around six? You can show me your shots, and we can discuss the angles."

"The angles?" Maria asked when Rory was out of earshot.

"The angles he can use to tell his story. He needs a slant that goes with his brand. I've been mentoring him a bit. It's fun, and he's going to teach me to use some of the software he knows. And it's been nice to speak to a person the same age as my children. It makes me feel a bit closer to them somehow."

Maria reached over and squeezed her arm, and Belle cleared her throat.

"Looks like it might be time to leave." Maria followed Belle's gaze to where members of their tour group were now gathering a few meters away. The tour guide who had left them to their own devices for the past forty minutes had reappeared and seemed to be counting heads.

They walked toward the group.

"So, what do you think about sharing a grandchild with Nathan?" Belle asked as they approached.

Maria stopped and stared at her friend. "You know, I hadn't thought about it. I'm not sure how I feel. I'm not even sure how I feel about sharing a daughter with the man. Especially when he hasn't told his son about her."

"I know. I almost said something, but Nathan probably wants to tell him. It will mean sharing personal information. Maybe he hasn't figured out how yet."

"I just hope he's not ashamed of her. I told her about him, said we could probably get together for lunch when the ship lands in Victoria, but now I'm thinking I should have waited."

"You can't protect Haley from things now that she's grown up, you know. It's not like she's a babe in arms anymore. She's thousands of miles away."

"I know. But she's still my baby."

"Yeah, and we would do anything to protect them, wouldn't we? Being a mother is a permanent job. Whether or not they're with you."

Maria saw the light in her friend's eyes dim a little, and she was happy to see the bus come up the street so she could turn her focus elsewhere.

"Ready to get back to our air-conditioned life?"

Belle grinned. "I sure am. It's been a great day, but I could really use a shower."

CHAPTER 18

Nathan slowly made his way on deck, careful to keep his foot up. He had left his crutches on board in favor of using his walking cast and cane all day, and he was now regretting that decision. His leg throbbed and if he weren't so hungry and hadn't promised to meet Rory for the barbecue, he would have stayed in the cabin.

The deck where the barbecue was being held was scattered with tables, all of which were occupied. He scanned the area for Rory and a place to sit and saw Maria nearby, sipping a glass of wine at an empty table. On the other side of the deck, Rory was talking to Belle, so he guessed they were likely dining together again.

He approached Maria, and when she looked up to

see who was casting a shadow over her table, he asked, "May I join you?"

"Certainly." She waved her hand at the chair opposite and watched as he eased himself into it. She took another sip of her drink and seemed to search for something to say. Finally, she asked, "What happened to your leg?"

Ah, a safe topic. Good. "I was trying to get a picture of a Verreaux's eagle when I was hiking in South Africa a few months ago. Got the shot, but then I slipped and fell down the side of a hill. Rory and our guide took turns dragging me down the mountain on a stretcher."

She winced. "How long did that take?"

"About three hours, and then I had to be taken to the hospital in Cape Town, where they operated on me. Thank goodness for Rory."

"He's a good kid."

"Yes. He's independent, adventurous, but he still looks after his old dad. His mother did a good job. I just wish I had been there more."

"You didn't spend time at home?"

"I worked as a rigger, so I traveled wherever I was needed. I was usually in camp for two or three weeks, then flown out for a week or two, depending on the company. And while my mother was alive, I would spend a week every three months on the island. When I was away, Ramona took on the largest share of raising the boys. It got so that when I was home, I was just in the way. Ramona had a routine, and I messed it up."

"I've heard it's hard when one person works away. A friend of mine is married to a navy man."

"Exactly. Anyway, a few years ago, she met Zane. Ironically, that was just about the time I got an office job at HQ. I had learned to manage projects and I could do that from Toronto, but it was all too little too late. Trevor still hates me for not being there. Apparently, Zane is not his favorite person. And Rory thinks I'm a lost cause who can't commit to a relationship." He glanced toward his son and smiled.

"But I am glad Ramona found someone who could make her happy. I never could. And after she left, I realized maybe I wasn't happy with her either. Perhaps that's why I was always away."

The silence descended between them again. Had he said something wrong? Maybe she didn't respect his decision to work in camps to support his family while leaving Ramona to raise the boys.

Whatever it was, she seemed distant compared to the day before. That spark of what had felt like attraction was missing. He should have found her again, talked things through. But instead, he'd done just what Rory accused him of. He'd run away from the issue.

"Have you told him about Haley?"

Her question startled him. He would have preferred to discuss the unspoken energy between them, the way the tilt of her head and the curve of her lips made him want to move closer, but she was probably right to keep to safer topics.

"No. I'm waiting for the right time. It would be best if Trevor were here too, but since that's not possible, I'll have to tell them separately."

"I told Haley you were here. That you'd like to meet her."

"And how did that go?" He watched her face, eager for the answer. Another child to get to know. The idea scared the devil out of him.

"She was excited. She has a lot of questions, of course. I told her maybe we could set up a call before we get there. Or a video call. You could meet her that way first. If you're ready, of course. "

"I'd like that."

"Could we do it in the evening on our next sea day, if she's available? After dinner, maybe?"

He nodded.

"She'd also like a picture of you and Rory and

Trevor if you have one you can share."

"If you give me your email address, I'll send you some."

She pulled a pad of paper out of her small purse and wrote down the information.

"Thank you." He took the paper from her and held her gaze. Her tongue darted out to dampen her lips. Did her tongue still taste like strawberries? Probably not. But it would be nice to know for sure. And her lips. Were they still soft as velvet?

"Listen, there's something else you need to know." He focussed on those lips and then on what she was saying.

"Yeah? What's that?"

"Haley told me she's pregnant. She and her fiancé are expecting a baby in seven months."

"Maria's going to be a grandmother, Dad. Isn't that great?" Rory came up behind him and slapped him on the back. "I told her if you're waiting for me to give you grandchildren, you'll be waiting a long time. But Trev might get there eventually. He likes kids. I just like being one."

Nathan looked from Maria to Rory, unsure of what to say. He wanted to celebrate this news. Like a father would.

The idea of being a grandfather was exciting. He

loved the idea. To know a child from when they were born. To be there for all the important events in their lives, unlike when he was a father, forced to work away for so many years.

But making that idea into reality was going to take time. To get to know this baby, he would have to get to know Haley. And right now, the only way to do that was by gaining Maria's trust.

She was looking at him carefully, as though she were worried about something, and he realized he had said nothing. Hadn't reacted to the news.

"That is wonderful news, Maria. I know you will be a wonderful grandmother." There, that was a good thing to say. She was smiling again.

Rory sat down beside Maria and started scrolling through his phone, talking about all the pictures he had taken that day and the blogging advice Belle had given him: how to talk about the details and the off-the-beaten-path experiences.

Nathan listened with half an ear and nodded at what he hoped were appropriate times, all the while looking at Maria with what he was sure was a silly grin on his face. A grandfather. He was going to be a grandfather. Maria was going to be a grandmother. They were going to be grandparents.

And the best part was that she was grinning back.

CHAPTER 19

Maria watched Nathan's face light up and couldn't help returning his smile. He was happy about being a grandfather. Most of the fear and anxiety about inviting this near stranger into her daughter's life, slipped away.

He was happy, and it reminded her of the old Nathan. The one she had known as a teenager. The one she had watched from afar for two years before he finally noticed her. The one who had, in fact, changed her life irrevocably with his love. Not just by the pregnancy that resulted from their union, but by seeing beyond her shyness and uncertainty, her need to always be careful and watchful and acceptable, and waking her up to possibilities. He helped her be seen. Enough, perhaps, that Evan finally saw her as a woman rather than the girl next door.

All those things that Evan had appreciated about her—her sense of adventure, her intelligence, her creativity—had been appreciated by Nathan first. He had been the first to love her for herself, and for that she would always be grateful.

Watching him with Rory also gave her confidence that he would treat her daughter—their daughter—well.

But would he be there? He hadn't been there much for Rory during Rory's formative years. He hadn't stuck with his marriage. And Maria couldn't forget he hadn't fought for her, either, when he thought she was seeing Evan. Could he commit to a long-term relationship with Haley? Or would he ultimately abandon her, too?

The only way she would know for sure was to spend more time with him over the next few days. Get to know him again.

When there was a break in Rory's monologue, she asked, "Do you think it would be okay for me to tag along with you tomorrow while you're taking pictures of the canal?"

Nathan's face lit up. "Absolutely! I'm glad you're still taking pictures. You had a great eye when you were younger."

"Not quite like yours, but I try to improve a bit

each year," she said.

"Don't compare yourself to others, Maria. Everyone has a different view of the world, and I have learned through all my years of teaching that beauty and storytelling are unique to everyone."

Huh, she hadn't thought of it that way before. "I'll try to remember that." His eyes were still holding hers, and she saw him there: the old Nathan. The one who always found the value in others. The one she had once loved with all her being.

"Ahem." Rory cleared his throat, and she tore her gaze away from Nathan's. Rory was watching them, a strange expression on his face.

"I think the food is ready," he said. "Did you want me to get you a plate, Dad?"

"That would be great, Rory. My leg hurts like the devil today."

"I'll come with you." Maria jumped up, wanting to put a distance between her and Nathan. Being beside him was like finding a campfire after a long trek on a cold winter's night, and she couldn't trust herself not to get too close, to not get burned.

They rose, leaving Nathan behind at the table. Rory motioned for her to go first in the line, and she stepped ahead. But she was startled when she heard Rory say in a low voice, "He's vulnerable right now."

Had she heard him? Was he talking to her? "Pardon?" She spun to look at him.

"He has a lot going on. His accident was worse than he lets on. I don't think he'll be able to hike all over the world like he once did."

"That's a hard transition, giving up what you love." She turned again to take another step forward in the line, careful not to collide with the woman ahead of her.

"I'm just asking you to please be careful with him." His voice was low, like Nathan's, and the words crept through the air to the back of her neck, raising hairs there. If she closed her eyes, she could remember his father doing... No, she had to stop that thought. It was the precise reason she had walked away from the table.

"I'm not sure what you're saying, Rory."

"I've never seen my dad look at a woman like he looks at you. Not even my mother. Please don't hurt him again." She whirled to face him again.

"Is that what he told you? That I hurt him?" She felt anger bubble in her chest like a cauldron overheating.

"He didn't have to. It's the way he says your name, the sadness in his eyes when he saw you walk away from the table that first day. I know my dad. And I know when he's hurting."

His words were like cold water added to an overheating brew, and her anger cooled a little.

"Not that it's really your business, but there's more to this story than you know, and he wasn't the only one who was devastated when he left. It took me years to get over Nathan." And if she were honest with herself, she'd never quite succeeded in kicking him out of her heart.

Rory looked chastened. Good. She hoped that would shut him up for a bit. Though the boy knew how to talk. She turned her back on him again and stepped forward to pick up a plate and focus on filling it with salad and a little of the barbecued meat.

When she returned to the table, she was pleased to see Belle had joined Nathan and was speaking animatedly to him. Maria nodded to her friend and slid quietly back into her seat, carefully placing the serviette over her lap, and focusing on her plate. When Rory returned with Nathan's plate, Belle accompanied him to the buffet, leaving Maria and Nathan alone again. Eating in silence.

"I'll probably turn in after dinner," he said. "Get some rest. We're meeting on the top deck at dawn."

"That's early," she said.

"Yes, but we want to get shots of us going into the canal. The approach. The sunrise."

"I'll see you at dawn, then," she said, returning her gaze to the food and spearing salad with her fork.

"Looking forward to it," he said after a moment, and she looked up to meet his gaze again. Damn those eyes. Her throat was dry again, so she reached to her right to grab her drink and take a sip. All the while her eyes stayed on his, as though they were magnetized, and she couldn't look away.

"Did you want to catch the show tonight?" Belle's voice broke the connection, and Maria turned to catch a smirk on her friend's face.

"I'm going to go to my room after dinner," she said. "All the walking today has tired me out, and Nathan just told me we're meeting at dawn to take pictures."

"The entire class is meeting," Nathan corrected, possibly because he saw the look on Rory's face now, too. They both looked like high-school students who had caught their teachers dancing on tables in the local pub. Puzzled, fascinated, shocked, bemused. "I'm going back to the room early as well. My leg is killing me."

Rory frowned at that last remark. The boy really cared about his father. It was good to see they had such a strong bond.

"Well, since Dad's bailing on me, do you mind if I go to the show with you?" Rory asked. "And there's a bunch of people meeting up at the bar afterward. You could join us."

Belle turned to smile at Rory. "That sounds like fun."

They spent the rest of the meal reflecting on the day, the conference, and their plans for the next day—and all the while, Maria was aware of Nathan. His voice, his smile, his calm way of explaining concepts to them. She could have listened to him all evening, but eventually they had lingered over coffee and dessert long enough, and Rory and Belle got up to leave.

"See you later, Dad," said Rory. "You okay to get back to the room alone?"

He glanced Maria's way on the word *alone*, and Maria calmly returned his glance, as though she hadn't heard his warning to stay away from his father. The cheek of the boy.

They watched them go. "I guess I should get going, too," Nathan said.

"Yes. We should get going."

"If you aren't too tired, I wonder, could I take you up on the offer you made the other day to show me more pictures of Haley?"

Her heart jumped, and she wanted to leap from

her chair in anticipation. Instead, she calmly answered, "Yes, I have some time."

They walked down the deck, and when they boarded the elevator, he leaned forward on his crutches, watching her with those eyes again.

"I have some from when she was a baby all the way through to last month. It may take a while."

"If we can't get through them all today, we may have to set another time." His voice was soft, a whisper, and she got that wrong idea again. She stepped away from him when the elevator got to her floor and led him down the hall to her cabin.

When he'd entered her room with his crutches and she'd closed the door behind them, he paused in front of her and leaned closer. "I've never forgotten you, Maria."

Maria had a large stateroom compared to others due to her loyalty to the cruise line, but Nathan's presence seemed to fill it completely. She was trapped between him and the door now, wanting to flee yet wanting desperately to stay.

"I've never forgotten you either, Nathan." She stepped away from him, not sure how to react, and walked to the desk where she'd left her laptop. When she turned around, he had settled into the loveseat, so she would have to join him if she were to show him pictures. Better than the bed, she supposed.

They sat together as she flipped through Haley 's childhood and told him stories about their daughter. He listened, asked thoughtful questions, noticed details, and continued to fill the room with electricity.

When they got to the present day an hour later, she closed the laptop and was about to stand when he said, "Would you mind if I kissed you? Or is that inappropriate?"

Yes, yes, yes, her body said. *No, no, no*, a voice in her head screamed. Her body won. She nodded, and he pulled her into his arms, his lips taking hers with a hunger that said, *I want you. So much.*

She returned the intensity of the kiss, pulling his head toward her, moving her body closer. Her need for his touch overwhelmed her need for reason.

They kissed a long time, exploring awakening needs she hadn't felt in years and unearthing memories long buried. After years of drifting, in his arms she felt like she was finally, finally, finally home.

She needed to be closer. His hands moved up her back, under her shirt, to the fastening of her bra. This was going too fast. Way too fast. She barely knew this man as he was now. They needed to slow down, and, judging from where his hands were heading, she needed to be the one to stop it.

She pulled away just as he released the hooks. “We need to stop.”

“Why?” he asked, reaching for her again, his eyes filled with passion.

“Because we don’t know each other well enough. I don’t want to complicate your relationship with Haley, and I don’t have any condoms.”

“Right.” He stopped and sat back, away from her. Shaking himself. “You’re right. We should get to know each other again first.”

“Yes, exactly.” He agreed with her. That was good, right?

“And I don’t want to complicate my relationship with Haley, either.”

“Good. Yes. It’s for the best.”

“But as for condoms… I have them.”

“I stand corrected. Good to know you come prepared.”

“So, I should probably go now. Thanks for showing me Haley ’s pictures and… everything.” He was grabbing his crutches, pulling himself to his feet, and leaving. Bad.

She stood too, keeping the space between them as small as possible for as long as she could. Her body was longing for his kiss again, but her mind was determined.

Mostly.

"Yes, you should probably be going. Rory will wonder where you are soon, and since he warned me off today, I don't want to get into his bad books."

"He what?"

"He told me to stay away from you. That you aren't in a place to start a relationship right now."

"Why would he do that?"

"I think he senses some attraction between us, and he's concerned. Maybe I'm a threat? I don't know."

"Well, I'm going to find out." He turned toward the door but stopped before he opened it and turned around.

"Maria, just so you know, I've never forgotten what you did for me. If it weren't for you and my grandfather believing in me..." He shrugged his shoulders. "I probably would have ended up just as my father predicted I would—on a slippery slope to jail."

Then he was gone, leaving her feeling both hopeful and terrified of what the future held.

CHAPTER 20

Nathan pushed open the door to his cabin and stepped carefully inside to a lighted room.

"I thought you were going to come right back to the cabin," said Rory, who sat on the couch, arms folded, with a grim look on his face.

Nathan stared at Rory and nearly laughed. Maria would have gotten a kick out of this, but he said nothing for a moment, just hobbled over to his bed and let the silence permeate the room before speaking.

"I spent some time with Maria," he said. "We went back to her cabin to talk."

"And what did you talk about?" Rory put air quotes around the word *talk*, and sarcasm crept into his voice.

"I would like to say that it's none of your business,

but it is. I have something to tell you, and I'm not sure how you will take it."

"Don't tell me, let me guess. You're in love with her. You and she are rekindling an old flame, and now you're going to join her on a cruise around the world. I thought after your injury you'd give up on always being gone. That you'd finally settle down. Get to know Trevor and me. But Trev was right. You're always escaping. You've never cared about us as much as we cared about you."

He swiped a tear away from his eyes, and Nathan stared at him. Is that what they thought? That he didn't care about them? That he wasn't there for them?

"You're not even going to deny it, are you?" Rory leapt to his feet and started toward the door.

"Wait!" Nathan said, louder than he intended, and Rory stopped, turned around, and stared. Nathan never yelled, and his son looked shocked. "Sit down. I told you I had something important to tell you, and I meant it."

"What?" Rory walked back and plopped onto the sofa, arms crossed on his chest, glaring at him as though he were a teenager and Nathan had just told him he couldn't borrow the car.

"It's about Maria. There is something you don't know about her that affects you and Trevor."

Rory glared at him. “Well? You gonna tell me or what?”

Nathan glared back, then thought better of a staring contest. He was the parent here.

“When I left Victoria to work in the oil fields, I had been dating Maria for over a year, and we... well. Anyway, when I left, unbeknownst to me, Maria was pregnant.”

“She never told you?”

“She tried to tell me. She sent letters, but I never got them.”

Rory rolled his eyes. “Sure, like she’d never heard of a telephone or internet?”

“It was the eighties, Rory. We didn’t have email back then, and phone calls were a fortune. I didn’t even have a phone number she could’ve called. And, when I left, she didn’t believe I would be back. I told her that I didn’t want to see her again. I didn’t know until two days ago that I have a daughter. Her name is Haley. She’s thirty-two years old and lives in Ontario.”

“You told me she got married right away. How do you know it was even your baby?”

“Maria did what she thought was right. She married another man. A man who loved her and her daughter—my daughter—very much.”

“Then why isn’t he here? “

"He died, Rory. Of a disease that meant he could never have children of his own for fear of passing on the gene."

"Wait a minute. Does this mean that you're going to be a grandfather?"

"I suppose it does. And that you and Trevor will be uncles."

"And you and Maria will become a family—the family with the woman you always wanted—and you'll live in Ontario near this new grandchild, and Trevor and I will be out on our own."

"Why would you even think that?"

"Because you always leave. Trevor said that's what Jake believes too. He said you just took off one day. Before your father left your mother, you just ran away for months. Never even said goodbye. You just abandoned him."

"Oh." He really had to talk to Jake, but that was something that needed to happen in person.

"Oh? Is that all you have to say?"

"I didn't leave on purpose. It's complicated."

"I'm not a child, you know. It's not like you need to protect me."

"Rory, there are things about this family that I'm not sure my brother knows about. I need to be the one to tell him. And he needs to understand why I did what I did."

"More secrets, Dad? Mom was right. You can't commit. Not to her. Not to Trevor. And not to me."

"Rory!" But Rory was already out the door, and Nate's foot hurt so badly, there was no way to run after him as he would have a year earlier. All he could do was go to bed, try to sleep, and hope he could mend things with Rory the next day.

CHAPTER 21

When Maria arrived at the bow of the ship after grabbing a quick breakfast, the deck was full of people holding cameras, cellphones, selfie sticks—anything to help them get a better shot of the approach to the canal.

She searched the crowd and found Belle with Rory on one side of the ship, but she couldn't see Nathan anywhere.

"Good morning," she said as she approached the pair.

"Hey, sleepyhead, come over here and see." Belle made room for her along the railing as she often did when she was first on deck. And as Maria had just as often done for her.

"Morning," mumbled Rory, shifting to the other side of Belle and not looking at her.

"Did I do something?" she asked Belle in a low voice.

"No. His father told him about Haley, and now he's imagining you and he will ride off to the sunset together and leave him behind."

"I see. Do you know where Nathan is?"

"On the other side of the bow in front of that huge group of people. He's giving a bit of a demonstration, but I decided to wait here. Too many people for me first thing in the morning."

"I'll do the same." She turned to the front of the boat, took the cap off her camera lens, and took shots of the approaching land, the locks, and the machines that would pull the boat along the locks and keep it steady for their journey through. In a few minutes, the guide would tell them all about this journey over the loudspeaker. She was ready. This could be her one and only chance to see this, and she wanted to enjoy it.

Belle and Maria spent the next hour pointing out sights to each other, laughing at shared jokes, and taking enough pictures to paper a wall. After twenty minutes, Rory joined in on their conversations and began to enjoy himself.

When Belle stepped away to go to the washroom, he finally spoke to her.

“Dad told me about Haley.” His eyes bore into hers and she nearly flinched.

“That must have been a shock,” she said, staying her ground, though the tension coming from him made her want to step back. “I know it was for him.”

“He said you tried to tell him, but he never got the letters.” He scoffed as though he didn’t believe it.

“That appears to be the case, yes.”

“Were you angry with him?” He was glaring at her. Why was he so tense?

“Oh, yes. Angry, hurt, heartbroken, all those things. But I married a lovely man who was very good for me and who I loved so much. We had a great life together, and Haley had a good father.”

“What about now?”

“Well, now we will move forward from here, I suppose. One day at a time. When we land, I hope I can introduce you to Haley and she and Nathan can get to know each other. She would like to know him. And judging by your relationship with him, I think he’d be a pretty nice man for her to get to know.” He seemed to relax a little, but he hadn’t finished his inquisition.

“Do you plan to keep traveling?”

“No. My sister’s husband is sick, and I need to be there for her. Besides, Haley is moving to Victoria, and

I will have a grandchild soon. I'm thinking of moving there. Getting a job. I'm not sure yet, Rory. I'm at one of life's crossroads."

"What about my dad?" Was he concerned about Nathan? Is that what this was about?

"I'm not sure what you mean."

"You aren't in a relationship with him?"

"Rory, my relationship with your father—at least the way you are thinking of it—is in the past. Right now, I just want him to get to know his daughter, so she knows who he is."

"Do you think you might like to have a relationship with him?"

"I think we need to cross that bridge if we come to it. Right now, I don't see any bridges on the horizon. Only locks. Look, we are starting to enter."

She pointed toward the first lock of the canal. The gates were opening, and the ship was moving into position. The opening looked impossibly narrow for such a large ship to go through, but as they watched the ship slid between the walls of the canal and moved into the lock. Maria took some shots and then stood aside to let Rory take his pictures. He looked up once he'd had his fill and smiled at her. Maria smiled back, relieved that the tension between them had dissipated.

Once the ship was well into the first lock, and they had listened to the navigator describe how hard it was to get funding to build the canal, Belle came by to ask if they wanted to get something to eat.

Rory said he would rescue his father from the marauding crowds and meet them in the café area.

"We'll try to get a window seat," Belle said, waving him off.

"Thanks for that," Maria said. "I think he has some concerns about his father and me, and what he feels could be our future."

"No matter how old we are, we still need our parents," said Belle. "And he is still figuring out life and his place in the world. He's quite unsure of himself under all that bravado."

"I gathered as much," said Maria. "I can see how a new sister and an old love from his father's past might scare him."

"*Is* it in the past?" Belle asked. "I get the sense that there's some tension of the sexual kind between you two."

"I'm not sure. I think it's more the memory of it. I've suggested we get to know each other again first."

"First? Did something happen between you?" Belle's face was as eager and interested as a seventh grader's.

Maria looked around to ensure no one, particularly Rory of the light feet, was around to overhear before she whispered, "He kissed me."

"Oh, my god!!"

"Shh."

"What did you do?"

"It would have gone much further, but I stopped it. I think we should focus on his relationship with Haley—and apparently Rory and Trevor, as well."

"But you wanted it to go further?"

"Oh, yes."

"Eeee," Belle squealed. "I have a good feeling about this."

"We'll see. It could just be nostalgia, or too much *Love Boat* as a kid—who knows? Meanwhile, I will get to know him."

"Oh yes, you will."

"For my daughter's sake, of course."

"Of course," Belle laughed. Then she pointed toward an empty table near the window. "Grab that. I'll get lunch, and I'll meet you back in a trice."

"Sounds good." Maria hurried toward the table before someone beat her to it and settled in to watch for Rory and Nathan, anticipating them like she had once anticipated Christmas.

CHAPTER 22

Nathan sat at the table across from Maria while Rory grabbed a plate for him again. He was tired of being waited on by his son, but more tired of the pain. He said as much to Maria.

"Have you tried sitting in the hot tub? I find it helps after a long day. They also have a great masseuse on board. I had a wonderful massage the other day."

"That's a good idea. Would you like to join me once we're through the locks and I'm officially off duty?"

"Why not? We can connect later if you like."

Rory and Belle returned then, and when Rory turned back to get his own meal, Maria rose to get her food. Nathan watched her go, then noticed Belle watching him.

"How did Rory take the news of having a sister?"

"Not well at first, but he seems to be coming around." Rory had caught up with Maria and was talking to her animatedly. He wondered what they were saying.

"And how about you? It must be odd to find out you're a father again—and that you will soon be a grandfather."

This woman didn't believe in avoiding tough subjects, did she? "It was a surprise, for sure," he said. "I wish I had known years ago."

"Why?"

"I've spent my whole life angry with Maria, and now I've found out it was all my fault."

"Life is a learning experience, Nathan. From what I know, Maria had a good marriage, so things worked out for her. And you seem to have landed on your feet." She winced. "Sorry for the terrible pun."

Nathan laughed. "You're a good friend to Maria. I understand she's going to return to visit her sister for a while. What will you do next?"

"Going home to chase my own ghosts," Belle said, then took a bite of egg and focused ahead to show that the subject was closed.

He watched Maria return, exchange pleasantries

with the staff, and finally sit down in front of him again. Her shields were also up, but he would thoroughly enjoy learning how to lower them. And he wasn't going anywhere before he figured out how.

CHAPTER 23

After a day of cruising through Gatun Lake, a protected artificial lake that preserved the water level for the canal, Maria felt at peace for the first time in days.

She sat on her balcony, making notes in her travel journal. Her grief counselor had recommended she start a gratitude journal, and later she transformed it to a log of her adventures: who she met, the things she did, the places she saw.

Today, she reflected, had been a great day.

She described how close the ship's hull had come to the wall of the locks, how the trains that ran along the side of the locks moved the ship forward, and how the gates closed behind them, filling the lock with water until the ship could sail through the next, higher lock and finally into the lake.

But she also reflected on how Rory seemed to have come around. He'd asked her at lunch about Haley, asked to see pictures, and allowed her to take a picture of him and Nathan to send to her.

"I can't believe I have a big sister," he had said. "I can't wait to meet her."

"She's meeting me for lunch when we get to Victoria," said Maria. "I hope you'll join us. She wants to meet you, too."

"Can Trevor come?" Rory asked, looking from Maria to Nathan.

"Let's ask him. But I'd like to tell him about Haley before that. I'm not sure how he'll take it."

"He said it explained a lot," said Rory.

"What do you mean? You told him?" Nathan's jaw tensed.

"I was upset," said Rory defensively, taking another drink, by Maria's count, his third beer. "So, I called him, and we talked."

"I wanted to tell him in person," said Nathan. "It wasn't your story to tell. And what did he mean by that remark?"

"It was my story too. She's my sister. His sister." He looked at Maria as though for confirmation, then blithely continued. "He said that it explained why you were never around. Why you never committed to Mom."

"Your mother and I had a good marriage for a lot of years. We just grew apart. What do you two do when you're together? Dissect every mistake I've ever made?"

"We don't dissect everything. Just what went wrong between you and Mom."

"I'm not entirely to blame, you know. Your mother had a part in it too," Nathan said.

Maria rose, not wanting to witness this personal exchange, but Rory waved her down again. "Don't go. You may as well know how we are since you're... well... Haley is part of the family now."

"Sorry," Nathan said. "You shouldn't have to hear this. Rory's had a bit more to drink than usual."

"You know, you have to admit it was kind of weird that you didn't get a job in town until after she left."

"It wasn't really an option until I had enough field experience."

"Come on, Dad. You know you could have found work in Toronto earlier."

"I tried, Rory. I tried several times, but the economy was bad, and I needed to get the training and hours as a project manager before they would let me take on some of those projects. And I had financial commitments that wouldn't allow me to just quit. I'm sorry if I wasn't there as much as you needed me to be."

"Did you really try?" Rory asked.

"I tried for several years, but it was hard to transfer to a headquarters office when they wanted me to train people in the field. It took me a long time to convince them I could be just as beneficial to them in Toronto as northern Alberta. Unfortunately, it was too late for your mom and me. I never realized how much my absence affected her. She always seemed so independent."

"She didn't have much choice," mumbled Rory.

"No, I don't suppose she did," said Nathan. "I wish I could change that. But at least I could be there for you and Trevor after your mother found Zane."

"I know Trevor was happy about that. He hated living with Zane." Rory paused a few minutes, taking another drink.

"It's all in the past now, Rory. We can only move forward from here."

"Yeah. I suppose so," said Rory, looking out the window at the view then back at his empty glass. "I'm going up on deck. Want to come?"

"I think I'll stay here for a bit," said Nathan. "I want to finish my coffee."

“See you upstairs, then,” grumbled Rory, and he walked off, weaving slightly.

Nathan watched his son go. He needed to talk to Rory about his drinking, but not today.

“Well, Maria, what say I take you up on that offer from this morning? Do you want to go to the hot tub?”

They met half an hour later, Nathan having left his walking cast in his room, and Maria helped him ease himself into the warm, bubbling water.

“Thanks. This already feels better,” he said. “I should have tried this days ago.”

“After about twenty minutes, you’ll feel even better,” she said. “And I’ve booked our massage for forty-five minutes from now.”

“A massage? I’ve never had one before.”

“It is definitely time you did.”

“You’re the nurse,” he said. “I’ll take your word for it.” He sank lower in the water. “Have to admit, so far, your advice is good. This feels fantastic.”

“Did you have time to call Trevor?”

“I sent him a text to let him know I would call him later tonight. He’s working right now.”

“What’s he like? Trevor?”

“He’s a lot like his mother, thank goodness. He plans, hates spontaneity, but he’s responsible and has kept Rory out of trouble while I was away.”

"You are also responsible. Maybe he gets that from you, too. You've spent years being responsible for your mother, for your family. Don't put yourself down."

"You're right. Poor kid got a double dose of the responsibility gene."

Maria laughed. "So did your other kid. Haley plans everything. Not to the point where she uses spreadsheets to plan a camping trip, but close."

"I suppose there are worse legacies we could leave our children."

"Yes," Maria whispered, aware that Nathan was holding her gaze in that way that promised caresses, kisses, more. She should get out of the water. Wrap herself in a robe. Here, with only liquid warmth between them, she felt vulnerable and at risk of breaking her word—to Rory, to Nathan, and to herself—that she wouldn't get too involved. She didn't want to be attracted just because he was a port in the storm of her indecision and change. Perhaps once she had a more solid plan for the future, she could see if the spark was still there.

Besides, according to Rory, Nathan had his own issues right now: his father, his accident, his need to find a new career. She didn't want to be a false lighthouse of hope that would bring him close only to crash him onto the rocks.

She glanced at her watch, hoping it was time to get out and move on to the next activity.

"Do I make you nervous?" he asked softly.

"Yes. I'm afraid of you."

"Afraid of me?"

"I'm afraid that my memories of you are getting confused with the present. That because we're both going through a lot of change, we might mistake the confusion for something more."

"And you're afraid I'll hurt you again."

She nodded, still watching him, wishing he would reach over and pull her close while needing to keep him away. "I think for the sake of the kids—Rory, Haley, Trevor—that it's wise if our only relationship was as co-parents."

"You're probably right."

"I am?"

"Definitely."

"Okay, then. We're agreed."

"You're probably right that it's not wise to pursue a relationship beyond co-parenting. But I've never claimed to be wise, Maria. So, if you change your mind, I'll be waiting."

She stared at him. Flummoxed. He had left the next move to her, and it would be up to her to define their relationship. She should have been relieved, but instead she was panicked. What if she moved things forward too quickly and ended with a broken heart? Worse, what if she waited too long, and he disappeared from her life again?

He watched her for a few minutes, as though waiting for her decision.

"How about we go get that massage? I'm sure it will help you feel better," she said.

A flash of disappointment passed across his features, but he rallied quickly.

"Lead the way. I would follow you anywhere."

She chuckled at that. "Be careful. I've gone to some strange places." Then she rose from the tub and pulled on a robe before turning to help him out. The last thing she needed was for him to slip and fall. That would not be wise, not at all.

CHAPTER 24

Why had he never had a massage before? He felt one hundred percent better. It gave him hope that physiotherapy beyond the basics might also help. It might even allow him to continue to travel and take photos.

He knew that Rory and Trevor would prefer he stay in one place, maybe open a studio, or teach as his mentor Sanjay was doing, but he didn't want to do that. At least not full-time. He wanted to continue to travel. But how could he do that and still build relationships with his children? He didn't want to be the absent or unreliable father. He wanted to be part of their lives.

Speaking of children, he still hadn't phoned Trevor, so after showering and dressing for dinner, he tried calling. Trevor answered after only two rings.

"Hey, Dad. You phoning to find out about Grandpa?"

"Partly. I also wanted to talk to you. I understand Rory called."

"Oh, he told you. I'm surprised he even remembered. He sounded pretty far gone."

"Which is why I wanted to talk to you myself. I was going to tell you when I got there, but perhaps it is better you know now."

"He said something about you finding an old girlfriend onboard?"

"Maria. Maria Phillips now. I think you'll like her. She's a widow, and she was the first woman I ever fell hard for."

"The way Rory tells it, you've still got feelings for her."

"Would that bother you?"

"It might have a few years ago, but since Mom married Zane, well, I don't want you to be alone for the rest of your life. I just wish you lived here. Rory says she travels a lot."

"Did Rory also tell you about Haley?"

"I didn't understand what he was saying. He was going on about needing to meet Maria's daughter because she was our new sister. Does that mean you're getting married again?"

"No. I just found Maria again. I'm not even sure she wants that kind of relationship." Though he hoped she did. He hoped she would see things his way. Life was too short to be wise and careful and responsible all the time. Sometimes you just have to dive in. Let go. See what happens and trust it to all work out.

"Then what was Rory on about?"

"What he was trying to say was that Haley already is your sister. Half-sister. Maria was pregnant when I left her, and I never knew until three days ago."

There was silence on the other end of the line.

"Trevor? You still there?"

"I'm here."

"Did you hear what I said?"

"Yeah. I heard."

"And?"

"I'm wondering what this means, I guess. Are we supposed to become one big happy family? Or is she just someone you'll visit occasionally?"

"I don't know, Trevor. I haven't met her yet."

"When do you think that will happen?"

"When the boat gets to Victoria, she's going to meet her mother at the docks and we're going to go for lunch. Do you think you could come?"

"I don't know. I'll ask Jake if I can get time off."

"How is Jake?"

"Still mad that you aren't here, but he's been like that lately. Always mad. I think there's something else going on with him."

"How about your grandfather? Has his condition changed at all?"

"They're moving up his surgery to later this week."

"When?"

"Friday, I think."

That was four days away.

"I'll see if I can get a plane from Huatulco. We'll be docking there in three days."

"Really?"

"Really."

"What about Rory's big break? He said he's learning a ton there, and they've asked him to teach a course for an online conference."

"I'll ask him what he wants to do. We've made a couple of friends here. He'd be in good hands if I left him to travel back on his own."

"Thanks for agreeing to come, Dad. Jake would appreciate it, though he may never say it. He's worried about Grandpa, and he's mad that he can't make it better."

"I'll let you know when I get a flight. If I can't get one from Mexico, I may need to wait until we dock in San Francisco. That's another three days."

"I'll tell Jake you're trying," said Trevor. "That will shut him up for a bit."

Nathan smiled at that. He wasn't the only one who found Jake's temper tiresome.

"And Dad, I'll think about coming with you to meet Haley if you really want me to."

"I do. She sounds like a nice person. It would be good for us to get to know her."

"I should go. I told Jake I'd close the garage tonight."

"Okay. And Trev? I'm really looking forward to seeing you."

There was a silence on the other end of the line, and Nathan thought his son had hung up. "Me too," said Trevor finally.

Nathan immediately pulled out his phone to search for flights. It sounded like Trevor needed him. He was still looking when Rory came in to get ready for dinner.

"I spoke to Trevor. Your grandfather's surgery is being moved up, so I'm looking for a flight back as soon as possible."

"But what about the classes?"

"I'll talk to Cheryl, the organizer, about changing the schedule in the next couple of days. See if they can front-load ours so we can still fulfill our obligation."

"Do you need me to come too?"

"That depends on what you want. I've told Trevor I'll be there as soon as I can. Your uncle is having a hard time with this, and it sounds like Trevor is taking a lot of the load. You can either come with me—or you can stay, complete our obligations as best you can, and join me when you get to Victoria."

"What if Grandpa dies before I get there?"

"I can't make this decision for you, Rory. But I need to book a flight as soon as possible, so let me know after dinner, okay?"

"Okay."

"Meanwhile, I'll see if I can find Cheryl. Do you want to meet me in the dining room? I reserved a table for six o'clock for the four of us."

"I can ask Belle what she thinks too. She gives good advice."

After speaking with Cheryl about the schedule, Nathan was confident that whatever Rory decided, he could still meet his obligations. He went to the dining room, passing men and women dressed in formal wear, having their portraits taken, and adding a festive atmosphere to the ship.

When he arrived, he found Belle and Maria waiting for him. Belle was wearing a tight electric-blue dress and silver stilettos, and while she drew many an eye, all he could see was Maria. She wore what his ex-wife had once described as a little black dress, and it hugged her curves in all the right places.

"Wow, you two look fantastic," he said, looking briefly at Belle then returning his full gaze to Maria.

"Thank you," said Maria. "You look nice too."

"Where's Rory?" asked Belle.

Just then, they heard a wolf whistle and turned to see Rory approaching. "Looking good!" he said.

Belle laughed and placed her hand on her hip in an exaggerated pose. "Why thank you, sir."

"Now that we're all here, let's check in," said Nathan. Using his cane with his right hand, he took Maria's elbow with his left and led her into the dining room, a move that felt as natural as if he'd been doing it for years.

"You're not using crutches today," remarked Belle.

"Maria made me get a massage and soak in the hot tub. I wish I'd done that days ago. I feel nearly new."

"It'll be hard to say goodbye to such an excellent nurse," said Rory.

"Rory," Nathan said in a warning tone. "What Rory is trying to say is that I have to fly back to the island earlier than expected. My father has taken a turn for the worse, and they've moved up his surgery."

"Of course, you need to go."

"I'll see Nicaragua and Guatemala, but I'll get off in Mexico. I've arranged for Rory and me to finish our classes early."

"I'll be sorry to see you go," said Maria. "But we can catch up when we dock, I hope."

"Yes. Unless something changes, I still plan to meet you and Haley for lunch."

"Well, we'd best enjoy the next two cruise days, then," said Belle. "Before we break up our little party."

"Cheers to that," said Rory, lifting his glass and taking a drink.

"What's everyone doing when we get to Nicaragua tomorrow?" Belle asked.

"I'm going into León with a group from the conference," said Nathan. "They have some great architecture there. But what I'm really looking forward to is Guatemala. I'm glad I will see Antigua before we leave."

"We'll have to go back to Mexico one day, Dad. Maybe Trev can come too."

"Do you think he'd like it? He always used to complain when we traveled."

"He just hated road trips. He gets sick in the back of cars."

Nathan paused. Why hadn't he understood that about Trevor? Had he been away too much to even know that his older son got motion sickness? What else had he missed?

"Well, if you think he'd like it, then we should all go together."

"Meanwhile," said Belle, "Rory, what are you most looking forward to about living on Vancouver Island?"

"Not sure. I haven't even decided where to live yet. Victoria is a decent size, and there's probably more opportunity there for work, but Trevor says the small-town life is pretty good with all the trails and outdoor activities."

"Sunshine Bay is lovely," said Maria. "I've lived there for years. It's where Haley grew up. And you're right—there's a lot to do there. I particularly loved kayaking."

"Really? My mother would never step foot in a kayak."

"There's a sailing and kayaking club you can join for a reasonable fee. That way, you can sign out a craft instead of having to buy one."

"Do you sail too?"

"Evan and I used to sail. He loved being on the water. We would often go to one of the islands and camp for the weekend, then sail back in time for work and school on Sunday night."

"That sounds awesome. Doesn't it, Dad? You can go on adventures in your own backyard."

"And there's a lot of wildlife to see. Everything from eagles and herons to bears, whales, deer, and otters," added Maria. "I particularly like watching otters. They are inquisitive and quite brazen."

"Hear that, Dad? Wildlife in our own backyard."

"I heard," said Nathan. "I heard."

Rory was doing his level best to make sure he had reasons to stop his world travels, but as Nathan watched and listened to his companions, he already had his reason to stay put.

Maria.

CHAPTER 25

The next day, in Nicaragua, Maria and Belle took a walking tour up to a coffee plantation.

"It's hotter than I thought it would be," said Belle as she stopped a moment to take off her hat and wipe her forehead with a handkerchief.

"Yes," Maria agreed, "but after all the food I've been eating this week, I'm happy to be hiking. And look at all these lovely red berries." She spread out her hand and gestured around her. "This will make great pictures for your blog."

"As will the selfie we are going to take when we get to the top," said Belle, starting to climb again. "We'd better keep going or we'll fall behind the group."

They set out again. "How are things going with Nathan?" asked Belle.

"Confusing. I'm trying to separate the feelings I had for him in the past from what I'm feeling at present. I spent so many years being angry with him for rejecting me that it affected the way I thought of myself."

"And then he shows up, and you learn that all those feelings weren't what you thought they were."

"Yes, and then there's the attraction I'm feeling. I don't know if that is based on my past or my present. As I say, I am confused."

"I imagine he's also confused."

"Especially after I told him he's going to be a grandfather! Did you see the look on his face?"

"All I saw was a silly grin. I think he's pleased. I hope it all works out. Keep me up to date, okay?"

"Don't worry, I will. We'll have to set up a video chat every week or so, so you can keep me up to date as well."

"I'd like that," said Belle. "I'm going to miss you, but I think it's time we both got off the boat and took another path for a while."

"You're probably right. Though returning is making me feel a tad guilty. Evan wouldn't have wanted me to be uncomfortable about returning home, but I am."

"Is that because of all the reminders of losing him?"

"Yes, but not in the way that you mean. I told you he ended his own life, but I'm not sure I told you how judgemental my sister was about it. Even when she joined me on the ship that time, she went on and on about how wrong it was."

"I heard her mention it a few times, yes."

"She acts as though somehow, I had been the one to decide. As though, by making him stay longer, I could have... what? Cured him? Evan and I saw what happened to his father. It was a horrible experience. He didn't want that."

"You were looking for her support, and all you got was her anger. Her pain. And probably her fear of her own mortality."

"She acted as though I wanted him to die. Do you know she never even came to his funeral? Yet she expects me to be there for her."

"I know," said Belle again, squeezing her arm. "And now you have to go back and potentially help her through her own grief process."

"Maybe that's what it is. Maybe I feel guilty about letting Evan go."

"From what you've told me about him, he lived a very

full life. He contributed to his community, traveled, raised a lovely daughter, and had a lot of love in his life. You didn't let him die, Maria. It wasn't your choice to make."

"And now there's Nathan back in my life, and I can't stop thinking about him."

Belle grinned. "Oh yeah? And what kind of thoughts are you having?"

"I wonder if he'll like Haley and whether they'll build a relationship. I wonder if his sons will like her. I wonder if he'll stick around."

"And...?" Belle stopped and turned toward her again. "There's more, isn't there? I've seen the way you look at each other. There's a mutual attraction."

Maria shook her head. "Okay, you win. Yes, some of my thoughts about Nathan are downright indecent. But I'm afraid to act on any of it."

"Because?"

"Because he could leave again. And what would I do then? Run away for another three years?"

"But Maria... what if he stays?"

Maria kept climbing. What if he did stay? Was she ready for that? After three years of living alone, did she even want another man in her life?

. . .

Twenty minutes later, they arrived at the top of the hill and asked a woman ahead of them if she could please take their picture. Together, arms around each other, Maria and Belle smiled into the camera, the mountain peak in the background.

"Well, whatever you decide," Belle said after retrieving her camera, "I hope you do it on your own terms."

"You as well, my friend."

"This may be the last time we climb a mountain together for a while, but know that if you are ever facing another mountain, figurative or otherwise, and you need to talk, I'm only a phone call away."

"The same goes for you. You have some mountains of your own to climb."

"Yes, and knowing you are there means a lot, Maria."

"And if you need me to come, call. Okay?" Maria laid her hand on her friend's arm.

Belle patted Maria's hand. "Thanks, Maria. I hope I don't have to take you up on that, but it's nice to know."

"Now, let's stop being so maudlin and start heading back down this mountain. I could use a good soak in the hot tub tonight."

"Lead the way," said Belle.

CHAPTER 26

Nathan taught his last class the day before they reached Guatemala, and he took some time for himself afterward, getting a massage and soaking in the hot tub in the spa. The spa was nearly empty, and he closed his eyes as he sat back in the water, happy to be alone for the first time in days.

Rory was great, but he was noisy, full of energy, and lately, since he'd learned about Haley, he'd been ruminating on what had gone wrong with his parents' marriage. Nathan knew what it was like. Hadn't he done the same thing for years?

There were people padding around the room in soft shoes and bare feet. He heard someone slip into the water, and another couple get out, but he kept his eyes closed. He had to rest—and think about what he was going to do now that he planned to move across the country. And though the prospect was painful, he had to face Jake and deal with his father after years of estrangement.

He sank further into the water, wishing he could just stay there, quiet, comfortable, away from all the feelings he was encountering: his own and those of his family. The only person he really wanted to spend time with was Maria. She had a way of calming him, making him feel better, making him see things differently. Maybe he should talk to her.

He lowered himself further into the water, completely submerging himself before surfacing. Time to get out. He opened his eyes to find Maria smiling at him.

"Enjoying yourself?" she asked.

"How long have you been here?"

"Just a few minutes. I didn't want to bother you. You were obviously taking a people break. I could leave if you like. I know what it's like to stay in a stateroom with another person for a week. Even if you adore them, it's still a lot of another person's energy swirling around." She used her hand to illustrate swirling; and he laughed. She knew exactly how he felt. Always had.

"You caught me. After living on my own for so

many years, it is a bit much to have people around all the time. Particularly when they all want to know something. Normally I enjoy teaching, but with all the rest that is going on this month…" He shrugged.

"And I haven't helped, have I? What a time to find out you have another child."

"No, don't say that." He shifted himself closer along the bench, so others didn't overhear their conversation—and because, to him, she felt like a spring rain after a long drought. "It has helped me understand why you and I broke up. I just wish I hadn't been such an idiot. I should have spoken to you. I should have fought for you. But I was young, hurting, confused about who I was. When my dad rejected me, I figured everyone would, and when I saw you with Evan, I assumed you had."

"I'm sorry you went through that, Nathan. I felt rejected then, too. My parents were so angry with me for getting pregnant they wanted to disown me. When Evan proposed, they forgave me, but things were never the same after that. We both did what we had to do and, by all accounts, we both had pretty good lives."

"Yes, I suppose we did. Though I screwed up my marriage, as you've heard."

"Long-distance relationships are tough," said Maria. "And I imagine your ex—Ramona, is it? —I imagine Ramona was lonely and left with a lot of responsibility. That's hard on people."

"After a while, it was like they didn't need me in my own home. She handled things, had a routine, and when I was home, I was in the way. I took on longer jobs to give her space. Seems I did the exact opposite of what she wanted."

"It's a fine art, isn't it? Determining how much space to give someone. Evan was pretty good at giving me what I needed and being there when I wanted him to be, but living alone has been quite nice, too."

"You like living on your own?"

"Most of the time, yes. It's nice to have my own space, but also to be able to arrange time with Belle or take an excursion when I want to."

"I can see the appeal of the cruise life from that perspective."

"Yes. You're together, but alone. A nice compromise."

"Have you thought about what you'll do when you go back to the island?" He held his breath, waiting to see if there might be a way to fit into her future. He desperately wanted to be in her future.

"I think I'll sell the house. It's too big for one person, and after years of taking care of all the things houses need, I'd like to try condo living."

"There are advantages to condos," he said. "I have one in Toronto, and I just lock up and go when I need to travel. I have a neighbor who watches the place. It's relatively worry free."

Her eyes lit up. "Yes, that's it. I want a place to call home but one that I can leave when I want to travel. It's an excellent compromise, isn't it? And if I want to garden, I can always use planters on the deck or join a community garden or something."

"And a lot of condos have recreation facilities. Hot tubs, gyms; a few even have libraries."

"Just like a cruise ship on land." She smiled. "Thanks. You've helped me solidify that in my mind. Now I just need to find a realtor, learn what my house is worth, and start looking around in Victoria for a condo."

"I know a realtor," he said. "In fact, you know her, too. My sister Sheila, who now goes by her married name Sheila Sales, is in Sunshine Bay now, and she's quite successful. She treats her clients well. I could connect you."

"Little Sheila is a real estate tycoon, eh?" Maria smiled. "I'd like to see what she can offer. Give me her number and I'll set up an initial meeting with her."

"Problem solved. What's next?"

"I need to get out of this tub before I turn into a

prune and get dressed for lunch. I've spent my entire morning here, working out, getting a massage. It's time to return to the people, I suppose."

He laughed. "May I join you?"

"Sure. Meet me in the dining room at one?"

"I'll be there," he said, before sinking back into the pool again and watching her get out. The pictures she had shown him earlier didn't lie. She still looked great in a bathing suit.

CHAPTER 27

As she showered and dressed, Maria reflected on her conversation with Nathan. Nathan of the broad chest that she had rather enjoyed looking at before he'd finally noticed she was there.

It had been nice to speak to him about her housing questions, and he had helped her find perspective. She didn't have to give up her freedom just because she was no longer traveling from one place to another every day. She just needed to find a place to live that she loved, preferably one near water and sunsets, and one she could lock up and leave for a few weeks whenever she wanted to go. That way, she could be close to family but still have the flexibility she really wanted. Maybe moving back would be easier than she thought, especially if she could sell her house for a good price.

She still had a few minutes before she had to meet Nathan, so she searched for Sheila's website. She needed to act before she thought about it a second time. That's what Evan had always said. Take the first step once you decide. It makes it more likely you will follow through.

She found the site easily and smiled at the tagline: Sheila Sales Sells. What a brilliant marketing angle. No wonder Sheila had kept her married name after she divorced. Maria typed her a quick message and sent it off before heading, as quickly yet nonchalantly as she could, to the dining room. She found Nathan waiting for her, looking relaxed in casual slacks and a crisp white shirt, with only his cane as company.

He smiled when he saw her, and she could feel that silly grin she had been trying to hide leap onto her face. Her feelings were now in full view of anyone who was watching. She was smitten, and it wasn't old feelings coming back and confusing her. In the few conversations she'd had with Nathan about family, about photography, about housing, she had found him knowledgeable, patient, self-deprecating, confident, and funny. He was an attractive man in every sense of the word.

"No crutches today?" she asked, giving him a quick hug as she would an old friend. She stepped back quickly before she embarrassed herself by lingering in his embrace. She so wanted to linger.

He shook his head. "I'm trying to wean myself off them. I hope tomorrow to do a walking tour with just my walking cast and cane."

They followed their host to the same table they had before. Was this to remind her to keep her distance, she wondered? Or was he hoping she would flirt again?

Well, he need not worry about that. She knew she couldn't give him more now. Shaking off her thoughts, she sat across from him in the booth. "Which tour will you be taking?"

"The one into Antigua. It's an all-day tour, but they assured me there will be a lot of free time, and there are places I can sit for a while and have a coffee. I should be okay."

"Maybe I'll see you," she said. "I'm going on a tour out there as well."

"And Belle?"

"She has more energy than I do. We went to the coffee plantation yesterday, which meant a hike up a very large hill. It was a beautiful day, but I just wasn't up for a bike tour tomorrow. So, she talked Rory into going and suggested I do a more sedate walk around Antigua instead. I understand there's a museum there that talks about the Mayans. I've always wanted to learn more about Mayan culture."

Nathan chuckled. "I won't be surprised if we are on the same bus, then."

"Why do you say that?"

"I think we're being set up. Rory was the one who suggested the walking tour."

"I can switch my tour if it makes you uncomfortable," she said.

He reached across the table and grabbed her hand. "Don't be ridiculous. I would love to spend the day with you." His thumb made little circles on her hand, and she swallowed.

She pulled her hand away gently and lifted the menu. "We should probably decide what we're having before the server gets back." She sounded prim to her own ears, and probably to his as well. She glanced up and found those eyes looking at her again. Deep and intense. A mountain lion waiting to attack. And all she wanted to do was roll over and play dead, making it as easy for him as possible.

"I won't change my reservation then," she said. "Now, would you prefer the salmon or the chicken, do you think?"

He smiled slowly, as though he knew he made her

nervous, before turning to the menu just as the server approached.

They ordered, and their drinks came, his an iced tea, hers a glass of Chablis.

"Have you heard how your father is?"

"He's stable. Sheila is keeping me updated." He reached into his shirt pocket and pulled out a piece of paper. "Here's her contact information and the number of a realtor she has worked with in Victoria, if you are thinking of looking there. Apparently, there's a newly renovated building near the water at James Bay she recommends looking at. The market is still hot, but there are a few nice places to be had there."

She took the paper from his hand. "Thanks for this, though I admit I already reached out to Sheila. Evan always said, 'Act once you decide,' and so it's become a habit, I suppose."

"You know, if he hadn't stolen the woman I loved, I might have liked Evan. He sounds like a good guy."

The woman he loved? "Yes, Evan was one of the best," she said. "I still miss him. Miss having someone to talk to about my everyday concerns. Like our conversation today in the hot tub. It was good to get another perspective."

"Glad I could help." He was looking at her with those eyes again, and she looked back, feeling bold.

The longer they watched each other, the more drawn to him she was. She was grateful for the table between them while also wanting to rip it away. When the server came to bring their drinks, she was thankful for the reprieve.

They ate in silence for a few moments, the air between them thick enough with communication that they didn't need words for her to know he still cared about her. Now the question was, what was she going to do about it?

CHAPTER 28

Nathan watched her pick through her meal and matched her cadence, though he wanted to gobble his food so they could leave and head to a more private place.

But would she come? She had said they should keep their relationship platonic, and she was talking about Evan again. Every time she mentioned that man's name, Nathan felt a blow, though he knew he shouldn't. But the old jealousy rose unbidden, and it was hard to tamp it down again once it was there in the room.

"Haley will be glad you are moving back to the island," he said.

"Yes. And in Victoria I feel like I can start again."

"Or we can pick up where we left off, all those years ago," he said.

She paused just as she was about to take a bite and put the fork back down on the plate.

"Do you intend to stay on the island then?" Her eyes were intent on his, and he knew his answer meant something to her.

"Yes. The boys need me, and now I want to get to know Haley and, if you'll let me, I would like to know you again. I still love you, Maria."

He held his breath, waiting for her reply.

She rubbed her hands on the napkin in her lap and took a sip of water before replying. "But after all this time, how do you know it will work? I don't want to complicate things."

"Maria, we aren't getting any younger." He placed his hand over hers and she didn't pull it away this time. A promising sign. "And as you say, we can start again. Clean slate. Together. Don't we owe it to ourselves to try?"

"And what do we tell your boys? Haley?"

"I think the boys will be fine with it. Rory's acting the matchmaker as far as I can tell. And Haley, I hope, would be happy for you to find love again."

She shook her head. "No."

"I see." He sat back, drawing his hand away.

She grabbed his hand again. "No, I meant, I don't have to find love again, Nathan. It's still there."

"Right then. We're agreed? Should we try again?"

She nodded, determined in her answer, then slipped her hand away again as the server approached their table.

"Do you want dessert?" she asked.

"Nothing on the menu," he said, smiling to himself as her eyes widened.

"Well then, I suggest we leave and find something more to your taste," she said. "There might be something on the room service menu."

"I could come to your cabin to look."

She drank the last of her wine and he slid out of the booth, standing in front of her to help her out of her seat. She looked up at his outstretched hand and then into his eyes before smiling and placing her hand in his. He wanted to leap in the air and click his heels before running with her, hand in hand, to the cabin, but he settled for sedately walking toward the elevators hand in hand.

When they arrived at her door, she let go of his hand long enough to open it, then pulled him inside and put the *Do Not Disturb* sign on the door.

He pulled her hand, so she stepped closer. But before he bent to kiss her, he said, "I just need to know that you're okay with this. It will change our relationship."

"As long as it doesn't affect your relationship with Haley," she said, reaching for him again.

"I think I can keep them separate." He pulled her close and kissed her, sinking his face into her hair, breathing in her scent. Then she was pulling her dress off over her head, grabbing at his shirt buttons, and helping him remove every stitch of clothing he had on. Together, they fell on the bed.

"You are as beautiful as you were at eighteen," he said, before they enjoyed all the passions they had all those years ago. Later, before he fell asleep in her arms, he thought, *I could stay here forever*.

CHAPTER 29

The next morning, Maria woke late after a difficult sleep. Because of her nap in the afternoon in Nathan's arms, she wasn't tired at bedtime—and that had given her time to second-guess all the decisions she had made that day.

Did she want to sell her house? Why had she contacted Sheila? Did that mean she was obligated now because she was Nathan's sister? And why had she made love to Nathan? Did that mean that she was now in a relationship she wasn't ready for?

She knew he wanted more. Was she able to give him more now that she had been away from her care-giving role for so long? Did that make her selfish?

At three a.m. she finally drifted off to sleep, determined to continue the path she had set for herself. She would get to know Nathan and take everything else one day at a time. She was not committed. She was exploring. Just as she was going to explore Antigua. Antigua! What time was it?

She glanced at the clock and realized she only had thirty minutes to get ready, grab breakfast, and go.

As she scurried, she collected what she would need for the day ahead. Identification, wallet, sail card, hat, sunscreen. Hair still damp from her quick shower, she closed the door to her stateroom, went upstairs to grab an apple and a pastry for breakfast, then rushed back down to catch the tour bus.

When she got to the meeting point, she was told that the group had already left for the buses, and so she ran down the gangway and sprinted. She couldn't miss this bus. Sure, she was excited to see Antigua's museums and architecture, but she was most looking forward to spending the day with Nathan now that he was no longer obligated to help photographers.

She handed her ticket to the driver just as he was about to close the door, and spied Nathan in the front, his crutches leaning against the seat beside him. The last couple of days of teaching and touring must have taken their toll on his leg.

"Sit down, madam," said the tour guide, pointing to the seat beside Nathan. He moved the crutches, and she sat quickly, embarrassed to be that person who held up the rest.

"Glad you could make it," Nathan's low voice rumbled, and she turned to flash him a smile.

"I'm sorry. I slept in. I'm really looking forward to this."

"Me too." And he took her hand in his as the tour guide began his narrative.

She squeezed his hand, happy with the sensation of being connected like this, and as the bus rushed past lush greenery and rural villages, she was drawn into the stories the guide was telling about their surroundings.

The stories of the Mayan people entranced Maria, and she knew she would need to do more reading about their history when she got home. Perhaps even return one day.

When they arrived in Antigua, the bus pulled to a stop beside cobbled streets lined with buildings from the sixteenth century. They followed the guide, who pointed out historic sites and again told the stories.

"I'll miss the stories most, I think," Maria said.

"What do you mean?"

"It's what I have loved most about traveling. Hearing the stories about other cultures: their history, their beliefs, their traditions, how they do things."

"I understand. It's what I like most about taking photos. They say a picture is worth a thousand words, and I think that's true if you do it well."

"So, you don't think you'll travel anymore? By the way Rory was trying to sell Vancouver Island to you yesterday, I wondered."

"Noticed that, did you?"

Nathan paused for a moment to listen to what the guide was saying. He took a few pictures, then leaned on his crutches to follow the group to the next stop.

"I'll have to stay in one place for a while," he finally said. "My leg hasn't healed as well as I'd like, and I need to get that taken care of. Then there is family, of course. The boys both want me to hang around longer. I guess I misjudged how much they would need me, even into their twenties. And now there's Haley, who I can't wait to meet. And, if she allows it, a new baby."

"And your father?"

Nathan scowled. "My father and I haven't spoken in years."

"I can't believe that. Doesn't he know how hard you've worked to raise your boys? He should be proud of you."

"For some reason, Dad wanted to believe the worst in me."

"Do you think he'll see you when you get to Victoria?"

"I hope so. My brother believes I don't see Dad because I'm a jerk, but after he left my mother, Dad told me he didn't want me around the kids and that I wasn't welcome in his house without him there. Until they were adults, I only saw Jake and Sheila at Mom's place. And Sheila was the only one who reached out and kept the connection. Jake sees me once every few years, when I come to visit. But I haven't seen Dad since my mother's funeral, and even then, only from a distance."

"It must be hard to go see him now."

"Yes, but if I don't, Trevor will have to deal with his grandfather dying, and his uncle's resentment of me, alone. I can't do that to him."

"And Rory? Does he know his grandfather?"

"A bit. I used to take them to visit Jake and Sheila, and they took the boys to visit their grandfather."

"But you never tried?"

"I know when I'm not wanted."

"Or is it that you think you aren't wanted?"

Nathan shifted his crutch under his arm while he grabbed up the camera from around his neck. He took a shot of the statue the guide was pointing out, then turned toward Maria. "What do you mean?"

"Have you ever considered that your father had spoken in the heat of the moment? He had a temper, if I remember correctly. And he was blaming you for things that weren't your fault. Maybe after all these years he's seen sense."

"He knew how to get hold of me. For years, Ramona and I even sent Christmas cards, birthday cards, and, of course, the boy's birth announcements, but he never reciprocated."

This was worse than she'd thought. She had thought that it had all been a misunderstanding, that Nate had jumped to conclusions the same way he had when he'd seen her with Evan.

She turned toward him and noticed his face looked grey. "Are you okay?"

"My leg hurts, that's all."

"Let's find a place to sit down. There's a café over there, across the square."

"That would be great."

They made their way over, navigating the merchants selling their wares to tourists, shaking their heads no, and forging forward. When they reached the café, they found a table just being vacated and sat down to order coffee.

"That's better," he said, and she noticed the color was back in his cheeks again. "Have you thought more about our conversation yesterday? Still planning to settle in Victoria?"

"Yes. I've also thought about my plans for the next few years—about maybe getting a job. Part-time so I can still travel, but substantial enough to be meaningful."

Nathan looked disappointed.

"You don't think I should get a job?"

"No, it's not that. I was wondering... I thought..." He swallowed. "I thought you might have thought a little more about us. Maybe our future."

"I thought that was obvious," she said, reaching across the table to take his hand. "I think we should try dating."

"You do?"

"Nathan, since you boarded the ship, I haven't been able to stop thinking about you. Especially after yesterday... which was lovely, by the way. You've learned a thing or two since we were teenagers."

"I should hope so," he laughed.

"You were right about what you said yesterday, Nathan. Life is short and we've spent far too long apart. I think we owe it to ourselves to see how this plays out."

He leaned forward, squeezing her hand, those piercing eyes watchful. "But you still have doubts."

"Small ones." She laughed. "Like whether I'm willing to give up my freedom and my solo life, how we will tell three children who have lost parents through death or divorce, and how I will tell my sister. But otherwise, no doubts at all."

"First, we aren't getting married or moving in together right now, so put that out of your mind. I've known people to live as couples in separate homes for years. They prefer it that way. Second, I think you already won over Rory. Especially if it means we're going to settle in one place. He sees you as an ally in his mission to get me to stay on the island. Third, they are not children anymore. My boys have had a few years to adapt to Ramona and me, and if you want me to come to meet your sister, I'll come. We can do it together. If you and I are together, I think we can face them and win them over. In fact, I know we can."

She placed her hand over his in what felt like a pact. "Let's do it, then." And when he reached forward to kiss her, all doubt evaporated.

CHAPTER 30

Nathan spent another day with Maria—including two intimate interludes in her cabin—before they reached Mexico and he and Rory disembarked.

"I'll see you in Victoria," Nathan said, giving Belle a hug and then pulling Maria in for a longer one.

"By the time I get there, Haley will be in town. I can't wait for you two to meet. Meanwhile, take care of yourself." She turned to Rory. "Look after him."

Rory glanced between them and nodded. "Always do," he said gruffly.

Then they were off the ship, in a cab, and on their way to the airport.

"Dad, you and Maria seem to get along pretty well. You haven't..."

"Haven't what?"

Rory looked at him closely, and Nathan felt himself blushing. "*You have!* Dad, I didn't think you still had it in you."

"I'm fifty-two, Rory. What did you think?"

Rory sat back and closed his eyes, settling in for the drive. "I'm glad," he said. "It's about time you found someone. I think Trev will like her, too."

"Is there anything about my personal life that isn't taboo for you two?"

"No, not really."

"Great. At least I'm forewarned that I'll be moving back to the island to live in a fishbowl."

"It's just because we care, you know. Otherwise, it wouldn't matter at all."

Nathan knew they cared, but it was always nice to hear.

Twenty-four hours later, after a long series of flights and stopovers—the only arrangement Nathan could find at such short notice—he and Rory finally stepped out of the Victoria airport where they caught a shuttle into town, checked into a hotel, and made their way to the hospital by cab.

"I hope we get there on time," Rory said, looking at his watch.

"We've done our best," said Nathan. "You even

took a shower in under thirty minutes, which is impressive."

Rory hit him on the shoulder. "Shut up," he said, but he was smiling. Nathan's attempt at levity had lightened the mood, even if it was only temporary.

They stepped into the sterile atmosphere of the hospital and asked for directions to his father's room. "It seems strange to be back in a hospital."

"Yeah, I know how you feel," said Rory. "When I took you in, I was pretty scared you wouldn't walk again. You were pretty banged up."

"I'm sorry you had to go through that, Rory. But I'm sure glad you were there. You were very resourceful, and I was proud of you."

"Thanks, Dad." The elevator stopped, and the doors opened. "Ready to face the family?"

Nathan nodded and walked down the hall to find Sheila and Jacob in the room with his father. At least he assumed it was his father. When Nathan thought of his father, it was as he remembered him: well over six feet tall, with broad shoulders and muscles from working on cars and trucks all day. He had not imagined this tiny man with a gray pallor, intravenous lines in his arms, and oxygen tubes in his nose. He stepped into the room while Rory hung back, uncharacteristically silent.

Sheila was the first to notice them. She sprang from her seat and crossed the room. “Oh, thank goodness. I was hoping you’d get here on time.”

Jake twisted to look in their direction, his face registering shock. Then he stood to watch Sheila hug Nathan and Rory,

“Nate,” he finally said, when Nathan came over to shake his hand. “Dad’s been asking for you.”

Nathan nodded and sat in the chair Sheila had just vacated near his father’s head.

“Hey, Dad, how are you feeling?”

His father reached for his hand. “Can you hand me that thing? I want to sit up and get a better look at you.”

Nathan handed him the control button, and he pushed it, raising the head of the bed so he was sitting up.

“Rory? Is that you, young fella?” said his father.

“Hi, Grandpa,” said Rory, stepping forward to give him a hug.

“Where’s Trevor?”

“He’s gone to the cafeteria, Dad,” said Jacob. “He’ll be back in a few minutes.”

“Rory, why don’t you go find him? He can’t have gone that far,” said his grandfather.

Rory looked at his grandfather and his father.

“The cafeteria is just down on the second level,” said Jake. “He’ll probably be eating breakfast. He left home early this morning to get here.”

“Okay, I’ll be back soon.”

When Rory had left, Nathan’s father grabbed his hand. “I need to talk to you before I go in there, son.”

“I’m listening.”

“We’ll get out of your way,” said Sheila.

“No, stay. You two need to hear this.”

His father gripped Nathan’s hand. “Son, I did a terrible thing to you, and I need to apologize.”

“What are you saying, Dad?” asked Jacob. “He’s the one who left us.”

“No, Jacob. I’m the one who told him to leave.”

“What?”

His father turned to Nathan and said, “I was in a lot of debt when I lost my job at the garage.”

Nathan nodded. “I know, Dad.”

“And I was under a lot of stress. Your mother’s drinking was taking a toll on our marriage. She had wild mood swings, lashed out at me, and then I found out she was gambling as well. Everything I had been working for was slipping away. When you got caught in that stolen car, I snapped.”

“Nathan got caught in a stolen car? Why hasn’t anyone told me this before?”

His father turned toward Jake. "You were only eleven years old. I didn't want you to know about your brother being sent to juvenile detention."

"He didn't want me to be a bad influence on you, Jake." Then he turned to his father. "It took me a long time, but I understand why you did it, Dad. You were cutting your losses."

His father looked even grayer than before. "Nate, you do not know how much I regret it. I should have been there for you. I knew deep down you weren't the one to take the car, that your friend Chad probably talked you into it. Knowing him, he lied to you. That kid was always in trouble."

"I had my part in it. I was drinking and when he told me it was his father's new car, I was stupid enough to believe him. I should have known it wasn't true."

"You mean your friend stole the car, and you got in not knowing it was stolen?" asked Jake. "Why did you have to go to detention?"

Their father looked at Jake and Nathan. "It was because I took my pain and anger out on Nate," he said. "I hope you can one day find it in yourself to forgive me Nate."

"But why?" asked Jake.

Their father turned to Nathan and said, "I blamed your mother for years for putting a wedge between us. When she said I wasn't your father, I went squirrelly. I was convinced that you and she were the same, that she had set out to ruin my life, deceived me into marrying her. I was angry, and I should never have taken it out on you. You were still a kid, a kid living through a very confusing time, and I abandoned you."

"Thanks for saying that. It means a lot." Nathan paused, then said what he thought his father needed to hear in this moment, as he waited for life-threatening surgery. "Dad, we might not be blood relatives, but you are still my father. You were the one who taught me how to work with tools and gave me the skills I needed to get a job. You were the one who raised me."

"Thank you, son," said his father. "I don't deserve your understanding, or all the help you provided over the years. I didn't really know how much you helped until Sheila told me a few months ago."

"What are you talking about?" Jake sounded angry now. "What help? Why have neither of you ever told me this before? I'm not a child."

But his father just continued talking to Nathan, and Jacob slumped in a chair at the end of the bed, arms crossed, scowling.

"I've been remembering things over the past few

weeks. I've had a lot of time to think here. Can you help me understand a few things?"

"Of course."

"When you got out of detention, you went to live with your grandfather, and you went back to school. How did you get the job as a rigger?"

"Grandpa told me I needed to work out my anger, and he knew a guy doing the recruiting."

"Ah. I wish I could thank him."

"He was a good man," said Nathan. "I will always be grateful to him."

"Who helped your mother? Was it you?"

Nathan nodded. "Riggers make good money. I bought Grandpa's house so he could leave Mom an inheritance. Then we set up an allowance for her so she couldn't spend it all at once."

"And the kids?"

"I told Mom I would only help if she paid for their education. I think she was happy to do it. I never knew about the gambling, though." He turned to Jake. "You aren't the only person they don't tell things to."

"What did you get, then? From Mom's estate?" asked Jake.

"I took a small amount and put it into trust for my boys. For their education. But the majority went to you. You needed it more than I did," said Nathan.

"Why didn't you ever tell me you bought the house? I always thought she loved you more. Wanted you more." Jake's voice cracked, and Sheila stepped over to give him a hug.

"Meanwhile, I was jealous that Dad wanted you and not me," said Nathan. "What a pair we are, eh?"

"I'm sorry," said his father, and they all sat in silence for a few minutes, letting the information sink in.

"What else am I missing?" asked Jake. "You helped Grandpa and Mom, and you made sure we got help to go through school. Anything else I should know?"

Nathan and Sheila exchanged looks, and Nathan nodded his consent for her to tell her story.

"I went to Nathan when I finished school and wanted to buy into a real-estate business. I couldn't get a loan from the bank without a co-signer, so he helped me. Then, a few years later, he helped me again when I got overextended and the bottom fell out of the housing market."

"That was when we started our side hustle," said Nathan. "Buying houses and renting them out."

"Wait a minute." Their father said from his bed. He turned toward Sheila, "You took a loan against that business to help me with mine. You never told me Nate was involved in that, too."

"Would you have taken the money if I had?"

He turned to Nathan. "Are you the one who said it was conditional on giving Jake a bigger part in running things?"

"Yes," said Nathan. "I'm sorry I interfered, Dad, but I made a promise to my mother that I would see the kids were okay. She had a lot of problems, but she loved her children." He turned to Jake. "Very much."

Jake was silent. So silent that Nathan began to worry.

"Okay, there is one more thing. I'm not sure if Trevor told you or not," Nathan said.

"What's that?" Jake narrowed his eyes at him. "What else could I possibly have missed?"

"A few days ago, I found out I have a daughter," said Nathan. "Dad, you are going to be a great-grandfather."

"What?" his father's eyes lit up.

"I was dating a girl in high school. Maria. Just before I went to work in the oil fields, we broke up. I met her on the cruise, and she told me about Haley, my daughter. I'll be meeting her in four days."

"A daughter," said Jake. "You have a daughter? What's the mother like?"

He sounded sarcastic, and Nathan looked at him sharply. "Maria is the one who got away," he said to

Jake, silencing his brother. "I loved her then, and I love her now."

"That's wonderful," Sheila said. "Does she share your feelings?"

"I think so," he said. "I hope so."

"I'm going to be an uncle again," said Jake. "What's the kid like?"

"Why are you being so rude?" Shelia asked.

"She's a nurse, apparently has a great sense of humor, and is getting married in a few months."

"Where does she live?" Jake's tone wasn't improving. His question came out staccato, like an interrogation.

"Toronto," said Nathan, aware that Trevor and Rory had returned to the room.

"So does this mean you're moving to Toronto?" asked Trevor.

"No. Haley is moving here. She and her fiancé both have jobs here. He'll be working in this hospital, in fact. He's an oncologist." Why did he feel under attack right now?

"Maria's not coming after you for money?" Jake asked.

"What? No. Why would she do that?"

"I can't wait to meet her," said his father, breaking

the tension building in the room. "I'm sure she's lovely."

"Well, you concentrate on getting better, and I will bring her around as soon as she's ready," said Nathan.

The nurse came in then, followed by an orderly pushing a gurney. They nudged the family to the side, closed the curtain around his father's bed, shifted him to the gurney, then reopened the curtain.

Rory and Trevor stepped forward first to wish their grandfather well, then Sheila gave him a quick kiss. "We'll see you when you get out, Dad."

Jake smiled at his father. "Good luck, Dad. I love you."

His father reached out to him. "I love you too, my boy. I'll be back. You won't get rid of me this quickly."

Nathan was the last to lean in and squeeze his father's hand. "We'll be here when you get out, Dad. We're not going anywhere."

"That's good to know, son. We have a lot of catching up to do."

They wheeled his father toward the operating room, and Sheila grasped Nathan's hand. "It will all be okay," she said, and he hoped she was right.

Jake watched their father until he was out of sight, and then he turned toward Nathan and Sheila. "I can't believe you didn't tell me. That you didn't tell me I had it all wrong for so many years. Why didn't you trust me?" Then he stalked down the hall and was gone.

"What was that all about?" asked Trevor.

"Let's go for a walk," Nathan said, bringing Trevor in for a hug. "There's a lot to tell you and Rory about our family, and I'd rather not talk about it here. Dad will be under for at least a couple of hours. We'll be back before he comes out."

CHAPTER 31

Maria spent the day in Huatulco, walking in the market, sipping fresh milk straight from a coconut, and later sitting by the sea to eat lunch and wishing she could spend the day with Nathan, yet knowing he was where he had to be.

The next day at sea, she finally heard from him: brief texts to say he had landed in Mexico City, then Vancouver, and finally Victoria, where he was waiting for his father to come out of surgery.

Maria: Did you talk to him?

Nathan: Yeah. It went well. Better than I expected.

Maria: Good.

She smiled at that. Perhaps it would all work out with his father after all. Time had a way of giving things perspective.

Nathan: I'll let you know when he's out of surgery. Talk to you later.

It wasn't until the next day that she finally heard from him. Unable to sleep, she rose early, went to the gym, lifted some weights, and ran on the treadmill. She was happy to be back in her normal routine, but she missed Nathan, too. In only a few short days, he had become an important part of her life again. Waiting for news about his father—her daughter's grandfather—was difficult.

When she finally received the text, she was having breakfast and coffee and reading the last few chapters of a book while she waited for Belle.

Nathan: Surgery was successful, but it will be several weeks before he can go home.

Maria: That's wonderful news.

Nathan: Yes. But he's not out of the woods yet. There was some unexpected bleeding during the surgery. They need to keep him for observation.

Maria: How does he look?

Nathan: Tired.

Maria: Rest will help. Don't worry until there's a reason to worry.

Nathan: Thanks, Maria. I must go now. Jake has finally agreed to go with me for a coffee. He's been difficult, and I have some smoothing over to do.

Maria: Keep me informed.

Nathan: Sounds good.

"Is that Nathan?" Belle asked, throwing her sweater over the chair opposite and sitting down to drink the coffee she'd brought with her to the table.

"Why do you ask?"

"It's the way you're smiling. I've never seen you smitten before. It's kind of cute."

Maria waved her hand. "I am not cute," she said. "But yes, it's Nathan. His father's surgery was successful, but they are keeping him for observation."

"Promising news, then," said Belle. "Has Haley arrived in Victoria yet?"

"No, they're still in Alberta. Apparently, they got a flat tire and had to wait until the next day to get a spare. Lance didn't want to drive through the Rockies without one."

"Better to be safe than sorry. And they'll still be there before we are."

"Yes, but enough about me. What are you up to today?"

"There are a few people who want to learn about search engine optimization. I told them I'm not an expert, but I can tell them what I know."

"I'm sure that will be enough to help someone. Everyone has to start somewhere, and you know more than you did when you began."

"True." Belle nodded in agreement. "What about you?"

"I'm going to do some research into a course I've been thinking about."

"Do tell."

"Actually, it's Nathan who got me thinking about it. I'm not interested in going back to nursing in a hospital, at least not on the wards, but I still have something to contribute, so I'm thinking about mental health and addictions counseling."

"That sounds perfect for you. You're patient, you listen, and you already have a nursing background."

Maria sighed in relief. "I'm so glad you see it, too. I

was thinking it may be too late to start a new career, but the more I think about it, the more I think I can make a difference. I'm going to explore the idea, do some research."

"As far as I'm concerned, you'd be good at anything you tried. But this would be perfect, and heaven knows it's a field that needs good people."

"Thanks for the vote of confidence. I've found a course online. All I need is to find a local organization to give me a practicum."

The cruise director came onto the ship's intercom and announced a painting class that was starting at nine. Belle looked at her watch and downed the last bit of her coffee. "Gotta go. Talk to you at dinner. The show tonight sounds good. Want to go?"

"Sure. See you soon."

The next day was a shore day in Cabo San Lucas. Belle and Maria split their day between a visit to a glass factory and a horseback ride along the beach. They finished their evening by sharing a meal and comparing notes with other conference participants. This was another thing Maria would miss most about cruise life: meeting new people from all over the world every day. But the more she thought about her plans to stay ashore, study, and, of course, reconnect with

Haley and Nathan, the happier she was with her decision. She just wished Belle could be part of it.

San Francisco was their last shore day, and as they sailed in under the Golden Gate Bridge in the early morning, Maria was on deck to take pictures and send some to Nathan. He responded that he wished he could be there, but that his father was looking a little better.

When they landed, Maria and Belle took their last excursion together, both a little subdued. While they bused across the Golden Gate Bridge to see the redwood forests at Muir Woods, Belle voiced what Maria was feeling.

"I'm going to miss you, Maria. I've never had a friend like you before."

"I'll miss you too," said Maria. "But we'll stay in touch. I promise."

They walked through a stand of redwoods hundreds of years old while several others headed straight for the souvenir shop. "Look, there's a deer over there," Belle whispered, and she pointed into the brush.

Maria nodded, picked up her camera, and took a shot. "It's beautiful. I'd forgotten how peaceful it is to walk through the woods on the west coast."

"Sounds like you're getting your land legs again."

It was true. As they walked in silence under the canopy of the ancient trees, her quick transition surprised her. But it felt right. The closer she got to British Columbia, the more she felt like she was going home.

CHAPTER 32

"You any good at this game?" Nathan asked Jake, bending over the pool table in the pub where they'd had lunch and taking the first shot. Balls scattered around the table, but none sank. "It's been a while since I played."

"I'm not bad. Been getting a lot more practice recently." Jake walked around the table and bent over the cue ball, aiming at a striped ball, and easily sinking it. He then sank the next three balls before finally missing, giving Nathan a turn.

"Not bad. What made you start playing more?" Nathan aimed at a solid ball and sank it. There, at least he could still do that.

"Look, Sheila doesn't know. No one does, really."

"Know what?" Nathan asked, taking careful aim at the next ball instead of looking Jake in the eye. He took the shot and watched the ball collide with another and ricochet around the table. "That one almost went in."

"Val and I are separated. That's why she hasn't been to the hospital. I moved out about six months ago, right after Danny left for university."

"I'm sorry to hear that," said Nathan. "Why don't you tell Sheila?"

"Because I didn't need her trying to interfere. She has a habit of doing that."

"Was it your choice to leave?"

"It was Val's. I don't even understand what happened. And now she's dating a guy she met at work. It's over."

"And you didn't even see it coming?"

"No idea. She just said we needed some time apart. That I needed to stop being so angry all the time." He leaned forward and aimed at another ball, hitting it hard and putting it into the pocket with a satisfying smack.

"Is that true? Are you angry all the time?"

"Yes. I've been angry with you for leaving, with Mom for not being there for us, and even with Dad because he just let it happen."

"I didn't realize you thought I had abandoned you. When I got out of detention, I had to repeat a semester to graduate and then I left for work. I didn't leave you. "

"I know that now." Jake bent over the table and aimed again, sinking another ball. "And I realize now that Val is probably right. I am angry. Have been angry for years. After all they put you through, why aren't you? How can you be so calm all the time?" He was aiming at his sixth ball, and Nathan was glad he hadn't put a friendly wager on the game.

"Here's something I've never told anyone," said Nathan, causing Jake to pause before taking his shot and look up at him. "When I first started working in the oil fields, there was a lot of money going around. A lot of guys worked hard, played hard, and lost it all. I started to go down that road. Just like you, I was angry. I had lost Dad, Maria, and I wasn't allowed to see you or Sheila for weeks on end. All my friends had left home to work or go to school. And Mom was off the rails."

"What did you do?"

"Drew, one of the older guys at work—" He laughed. "Okay, Drew was thirty-five, but to my nineteen-year-old self, he was old and different from the rest. He was fit. He had a family, his own house, investments. He had everything I thought I needed to get Dad to respect me. So, I asked him for help."

"But how did you stop being angry?"

"Drew found me drunk one night in Calgary when I was on a week out of camp. I was out of control. I'd just found out Maria had married Evan, and I picked a fight with a bigger guy who beat the pulp out of me. Anyway, Drew took me home, sobered me up, fed me, and gave me a place to sleep. The next morning, he sat me down and talked to me. Listened to me. Asked me what I really wanted out of life. I told him I wanted to learn how he did it."

"And what did he tell you?"

"First, I had to learn to control my emotions. For that, I needed to learn skills. So, he referred me to a counselor. The company had some on contract. And I learned conflict resolution skills."

"Val always tells me I need help. Maybe I should have listened to her."

"Think about it. I can help you find someone if you need it."

"Would you? I'll try anything. I just want my life back."

"I've always been here for you, Jake. You just didn't know it."

"Thanks, Nate." He bent back over the table, took the shot, and another ball plunked into the pocket.

"How long have you been practicing this game?"

"Every night for about four months. A friend recommended it."

"If you can get this good at pool in a few months, think what you can do if you learn some anger-management skills."

Jake said nothing, but he looked a little relieved. Maybe, after all the years of distance, Jake could learn to trust him again, and Nathan could get his family back, too.

CHAPTER 33

The ship docked at Ogden Point in Victoria at eleven o'clock, and Maria was packed and ready to disembark. Belle helped carry her bags, and moments later they were hugging Haley and Lance, who had come to pick her up.

"Mom, I'm so glad to see you," said Haley. "And Belle, you're here too."

"I'm just along for the day. I'm continuing on to Vancouver tonight."

"But you'll join us for lunch, right? I could use all the support I can get."

"Absolutely. This is my last meal with Maria for a long time."

"There's a seafood restaurant right by the harbor. We're meeting them there in about twenty minutes.

But first," Haley said to Maria, "let me put your bags in our car. We can drop you at the bus depot later."

"Bus?" asked Belle.

"I'm going home to talk to Cynthia in person," said Maria. "I promised I would come and stay with her for a couple of days."

"Once we get our place, Mom's going to stay with us for a while too," said Haley.

"Don't worry, Lance," Maria cut in, "I'm already looking for a place to live."

Lance laughed. "Maria, you're welcome to stay anytime." He hoisted her bags into the trunk of his car and closed the trunk. "We can walk from here in ten minutes. Belle might enjoy seeing the harbor."

"Perfect," said Maria. "Let's go."

When they arrived at the restaurant, Nathan and Rory were waiting, as was a young man who resembled Rory. Maria stepped forward and hugged Nathan, then Rory. "And you must be Trevor," she said, before performing the introductions. When she introduced Haley to Nathan, he asked if he could hug her, and Maria nearly cried watching them together.

Lunch could not have gone better. Rory and Belle shared stories, and laughter often erupted from the table, causing others in the restaurant to turn and look at them. Trevor was quieter than Rory but could carry on a conversation, and Maria listened as he and Lance connected about hiking, hockey, and surfing. But she was most pleased to see Nathan and Haley 's solid first conversation. She hoped that meant they had begun to bond.

"I think that went well," said Nathan, as they exited the restaurant. "Thank you for arranging it."

"Haley is glowing. She is so happy. I think she really enjoyed meeting her new family."

"What are you planning to do now?"

"I'm going to spend a few hours with Belle, and then Haley and Lance are going to pick me up and take me to the 5 p.m. bus. I'm going to see my sister. She doesn't know about you and Haley, and it's time I told her."

"I'd offer to drive you, but I promised Sheila I would sit with Dad. Jake had to go home for a couple of days, and she needs someone here."

"Of course," said Maria. "We can plan to meet in a few days. Sheila is going to show me some condos."

"I'll see you soon, then," said Nathan. Then he and his boys walked off. She watched him go, and though she knew she would see him soon, she wished he would turn around and come back.

After a day of sightseeing, Maria said goodbye to Belle on the pier.

"You are so lucky," said Belle. "I would give anything to have my family back."

"I know you. You don't take no for an answer. I'm sure you'll be able to put it right again."

"I hope so. If not, it won't be for lack of trying."

"Call if you need anything."

"I will," said Belle, before giving Maria a tight hug and walking back through security and onto the ship. Maria waited until she was on board before leaving.

She still had a few hours of travel before she got to Cynthia's house, and she didn't want to miss the bus.

As the bus approached Sunshine Bay, the wind picked up, bringing rain with it, and when Maria stepped down onto the curb, she could smell the sweet scent of wet earth and grass mingled with the sea air. "The smell is dimethyl sulfide," Evan had always remarked, laughing when she complained that knowing the science behind sea air ruined the romance.

She hailed a cab and felt anticipation as it wove through traffic toward her sister's door. The house looked the same, as though nothing had changed. But things had changed. At least she had.

When Cynthia opened the door, she looked older, tired, ungroomed, and distracted—until she recognized Maria. And then a tear formed, and a smile erased the wrinkles and lit up her face.

"You came," said Cynthia, pulling Maria into a tight hug.

"Of course, I did," said Maria.

"How long can you stay?"

"A few days, but I'll be close by as long as you need me."

Cynthia ushered her into Sabrina's old room, the one she had turned into a guest room. "Settle in. Then come and have tea. It is *so good* to have you here."

Maria looked around the room. It wasn't much bigger than her regular cabin, but the beige carpets and wooden bookshelves were a welcome change. Through the window, she could see flowers and grass and a bird feeder visited by chickadees and sparrows. No gulls.

She unpacked and wandered to the kitchen, where Gerrard greeted her as he always had. But Maria knew change may be coming. Whatever his prognosis, she would help Cynthia cope as best she could.

Around the dinner table, Maria told them about Nathan and Haley.

"Why didn't you ever tell me?"

"Dad told me not to. And after they died, it was easier to say nothing."

"What's Nathan like?"

"He's a lovely man," Maria said.

She expanded on his virtues until Cynthia finally said, "You still love him, don't you?"

"What makes you say that?"

"I know you, and I haven't seen you this happy in years."

"Yes, I do still love him."

"Does he know that?"

"Yes, he knows."

"When will you see him again?"

"I'm going to look at condos in Victoria in a couple of days."

"Victoria." Cynthia did not look pleased. "Why Victoria?"

"Haley is living there, and so will my grandchild soon."

"Grandchild?"

"She and Lance are getting married in a couple of months. Once I have a date, I'll let you know."

"You want to live in Victoria?" said Cynthia.

"I know you thought I would come back here, but I want to go back to school, start a new career, and spend time with Haley and the baby. I think it will be easier to do all that from Victoria. Of course, I will still visit."

"I understand," said Cynthia. "At least you won't be on a boat in the middle of the sea anymore. If I need you, you'll only be two hours away."

"Exactly." Maria was relieved that Cynthia had taken it so well.

"Maria, I need to apologize. I have had a lot of time to think, and I've been talking to a lot of people about caregiving in case Gerrard's diagnosis is a worst-case scenario."

"You always do like to be prepared."

"I didn't understand what you went through when Evan got sick. I really had no idea the toll it takes on the caregiver and the person being cared for. I understand now why he did what he did. I wanted you to know that."

Maria put her hand on her sister's arm. "It's all in the past Cynthia."

"But I didn't even go to his celebration of life, the one he held before he died. I am so ashamed."

"Don't worry. There were so many people there he didn't have time to talk to everyone, anyway. And he knew you loved him."

"But I wasn't there for you. I can't believe how selfish I was."

Maria smiled. Though it would have been nice to have the support earlier, she would take what she could get. Perhaps she and her sister could become close again. In time.

They talked for a few more hours and Maria finally retired, pulled on nightclothes, and checked her pockets for items before putting her clothes into the hamper. In her slacks pocket, her fingers found the shell that had accompanied her journey. She examined it from every angle before setting it on the table beside her bed.

She was finally home.

EPILOGUE

Three months later, Maria knocked on the door to Nathan's new condominium and shifted the weight of the large jade plant she was carrying up onto her hip.

When he opened the door, she handed the plant to him as she stepped inside. "What's this for?" he asked, taking it from her and bending to kiss her cheek.

"It's a housewarming gift," she said. "It should do well in a place where it can get some sunlight for at least six hours." She considered the room for a moment, her finger to her lips, and pointed to a table behind a couch near the window. "Like there, for example."

"Sounds good." He walked over to the spot and set it down. "What do you think?"

"That will work well, but don't over-water it," she said. "Once every two or three weeks."

"You can come and check up on it anytime."

"I intend to," she said. "Do you know how long it takes to get a jade plant that big?"

"Is this one that you grew?"

"No, most of mine died while I was away. Cynthia is not a conscientious plant-sitter, but I have grown many over the years. They are one of my favourites."

"I promise to do my best, though I don't have much experience in this area. Now tell me, what do you think?"

She walked around the open-concept room. "The flooring you picked out looks even better than it did on the sample, and I really like the green walls. It gives the room a calm vibe."

"Do you like it?"

"I do. I think this will make a very comfortable home. But the important question is, do you like it? You're the one who'll be living here."

"So far, so good. I love the balcony best; I can sit and watch the sunsets."

"I always love a good sunset."

"You're welcome to join me anytime you like," he said, reaching into his pocket and handing her a key. "I mean it. Anytime. You don't even need to knock."

She took the key from him and pulled him close to kiss him. “Perfect. Now I can check up on the plant.”

He laughed. “So that’s what you think this is? An offer for you to be my plant watcher?”

“I take plant watching very seriously, Nathan. I may need to check up on Jade there a couple of times a day.”

He grinned. “Or you could just stay.”

“I’ll think about it,” she said, walking around the room and glancing into the bedrooms and bathrooms. “I do love the way the furniture looks in here.”

“I had some good advice,” he said, laughing.

She twirled around to face him again and took a bow. “Why, thank you.”

“Now that my new place passes your inspection, are we still on for lunch and the tour of Rory’s studio? I’m a bit hungry.”

“Haley is meeting us in about half an hour at the Jamaican place downtown. She has a craving for ackee rice.”

“We should get going, then. It can take a while to find parking on Sundays.”

“Can we stop by my place first? I have to pick up a couple of things.”

“Of course,” he said, gesturing for her to walk ahead of him. “Go ahead. I just need to grab my keys.”

She walked two doors down the hall and entered the next condominium, an airy apartment that was a mirror layout to Nathan's but done in more neutral tones. She looked back to see if Nathan was coming, but his door was still closed, so she walked inside and grabbed her jacket, a baby book she had bought for Haley, and a hydrangea for Rory's open house the following day.

"Hey, you left your key in the door," he said, holding it out to her. "You should probably add it to your keychain, or you could lose it."

"That's not my key," she said, holding up her key ring.

"It was in your door."

"That one's for you," she said. "Just in case you need it for some reason."

"Like watering your plants?" he looked around the room at all the plants she had.

"I can always use a good plant waterer." She walked over and kissed him. "But I was thinking more of when you want to watch the sunset from a different angle."

"Does this mean we are now in a committed relationship?" he asked. "I need to let Rory know we are now officially living together, but apart. He thinks I can't commit."

"You know very well we are committed. I love you; you love me. We just happen to like our personal space."

"People are going to think we're odd, having separate places only a few doors apart," he said.

"But it works for us, so who cares what they think?"

"Exactly," he said, pulling her into his embrace. "It is the perfect arrangement, and it gives us more space for visitors when they come. Now, we'd best get going, or we'll be late to meet Haley. I'll lock the door." He held up his key.

"See, already useful." She laughed, walking out ahead of him. "By the way, now that you are all moved in, unpacked, and ready for your studio grand opening, what's on the itinerary for tomorrow?"

He fell into step beside her and threw his arm around her shoulders. "I'm not sure yet. All I know is that I plan to spend some of my day with you."

Note to Readers

I hope you enjoyed Repositioning: Lost Love, Found.

If you'd like to read more stories from Sunshine

Bay about friendship, love, and second chances in the second half of life, start with Love's Fresh Start.

To be the first to learn about my next story, and to get early access to content, and freebies, take a moment to go to my website at JeanineLauren.com and sign up for my newsletter.

And, if you enjoyed Repositioning, please consider taking a few minutes to leave a review. Reviews are a fabulous way to support authors so we can continue to write more books for you to enjoy.

Until next time...

Happy reading.

Jeanine Lauren

ABOUT THE AUTHOR

Jeanine Lauren is a USA Today bestselling author who writes stories about friendship, love and second chances in the second half of life, because let's face it, the second half is the most interesting.

Though Jeanine has been writing most of her life, many (okay, almost all) of her words have been for her day jobs, term papers, volunteer work, or used to make endless 'to do' lists she rarely looks at.

In 2019, Jeanine finally published the first book in her Sunshine Bay series -Love's Fresh Start - and is now writing as fast as she can, trying to make up for lost time.

To find out when Jeanine's next books are coming out, head over to her website at jeaninelauren.com and join her mailing list.

Jeanine lives in the lower mainland of British Columbia, Canada not far from the fictional town of Sunshine Bay where most of her characters live.

ALSO BY JEANINE LAUREN

Sunshine Bay

Love's Fresh Start

Come Home To Love

Angel and the Neville Next Door

A Sunshine Bay Duet (Love's Fresh Start and Come Home to Love)

Shops at Sunshine Bay

Christmas Trees and Mistletoe

Manufactured by Amazon.ca
Bolton, ON

34504977R00166